THE BOOK OF BONES

A BONES BONEBRAKE ADVENTURE

DAVID WOOD

ADRENALINE PRESS

The Book of Bones- A Bones Bonebrake Adventure
Copyright 2016 by David Wood

Published by Adrenaline Press
www.adrenaline.press

Adrenaline Press is an imprint of Gryphonwood Press
www.gryphonwoodpress.com

This is a work of fiction. All characters are products of the authors' imaginations or are used fictitiously.

ISBN-13: 978-1537279824

ISBN-10: 1537279823

BOOKS BY DAVID WOOD

Callsign: Queen
Destiny
Dark Rite
Primordial (forthcoming

Writing as David Debord
The Absent Gods Trilogy
The Silver Serpent
Keeper of the Mists
The Gates of Iron

The Impostor Prince

PROLOGUE

1871- The Badlands of New Mexico

"Beans again?" Carl tilted the brim of his hat down over his eyes and laid back on his bedroll. "Ain't we got anything else at all?" They were still days away from Santa Fe, days of nothing but dirt, rocks, cactus, and precious little water or game between them and their destination, and all they had left to eat were dried beans. Nearby, their horses cropped on a pitiful patch of weeds, and Carl found himself wondering what horseflesh tasted like.

"Not just beans. We got that jackrabbit you shot. Oh, wait. You missed, didn't you?" Little Mike let out a cackle and bared his rotten teeth. "Just joshing you. I reckon that critter was a long way away. Else you'd have hit it."

"It wasn't my fault," Carl complained. "I done told you what happened."

"You told me, but it still don't make no sense. You was about to shoot the rabbit, and a big-headed injun stuck his head up over a rock and scared you."

"I weren't scared," Carl lied. "It just surprised me is all. And it weren't no injun."

"A white man, then?" Little Mike kept his eye on the pot of beans as it boiled, stirring occasionally with his knife.

"It was gray. And it had a big head and big eyes." He turned over on his side and looked out over the open range. He knew how foolish his words sounded, but it was the God's honest truth.

Little Mike's voice suddenly grew serious. "Truth told, I've seen the same thing before."

Carl sat bolt upright. "You never told me that."

Little Mike nodded. "Last summer. I had about a dozen whiskeys, and when I went out to take a leak I seen somebody who looked just like that. Course, everybody looked that way for a while." He let out another cackle.

Carl felt his face go crimson. "You can go to hell." He fixed his hat, tugged on his boots, and stood.

"Aw, don't be like that. Sit yourself down. The beans is

almost ready."

"I'm going hunting."

"What do you think you're gonna find out there, ceptin coyotes?"

"I don't know, but I'm gonna look. Anything's better than listening to you." He strapped on his gun belt, turned, and stalked off into the darkness.

In the distance, a tall, rock formation stood dark on the horizon, and he headed toward it. Little Mike was right; he didn't expect to encounter any game. He just needed to clear his head.

Admitting what he'd seen had been stupid. It wasn't a lie, but nobody was going to believe him. Hell, if Little Mike opened his mouth once they got to Santa Fe, Carl would be a laughingstock. And when had Little Mike ever failed to open his mouth?

Somewhere in the distance, a coyote yipped. Several of its brothers answered its call, and a chorus of unearthly howls filled the air. Carl wasn't bothered. Coyotes weren't much of a threat. They tended to shy away from humans. Still, he touched his Colt, seeking comfort there.

"I wonder if you can eat coyote?"

The thought dissolved as soon as it had come. Something moved in his peripheral vision. Something much bigger than a rabbit.

Carl whirled and drew his pistol. His eyes searched the horizon. Cactus, yucca, and a single juniper. As he stared, something moved behind the large bush. He couldn't see much, but he could tell it moved on two feet.

"Who's there?" He couldn't keep the tremor from his voice. Thoughts of the strange thing he'd seen earlier flooded his mind. "Mikey, that you? You best come out afore you get yourself shot."

Nothing. Whatever hid behind the juniper remained still.

Carl dared a step in its direction, then another. Close by now, the rock formation seemed foreboding, sinister even.

"Come on out. I won't hurt you." Carl hoped he sounded more confident than he felt. Beneath the base of the juniper, he caught a glimpse of a bare foot—a foot with four toes. What in creation was it? Cold sweat slicked his lanky frame, and the night air seemed impossibly cold. The barrel of his Colt wavered.

"I won't tell you again. Come on out."

The thing didn't move. Instead, movement came from all around. He whirled, his finger twitching spasmodically on the trigger. The Colt boomed and jerked in his hand. He kept turning and firing, sending a bullet in the direction of every compass point, with a couple extras thrown in.

When it was empty, he stood in a thin, acrid cloud of his own making, and waited.

Finally, the thing stepped out from behind the juniper. Carl caught a glimpse of large, dark eyes, and he cried out in fear and alarm.

His mind told him to run, but his feet seemed locked in place. A dizzying feeling of disbelief swept over him, and his body went numb. Only the warm trickle down his leg kept him tethered to reality.

"What are you?" he croaked.

The last thing he saw was a flash of green light.

ONE

"You've got to be kidding me." Uriah "Bones" Bonebrake stared at the dashboard of his Dodge Ram 1500 pickup truck, watching as the arrow on the speedometer fell while the RPMs red-lined as he stepped down on the gas pedal. Not good. A green road sign loomed up ahead, and he coasted the truck to a stop in front of it.

QUEMADURA, NEW MEXICO 2 MILES

"Almost made it." He consulted his phone and found to his absolute lack of surprise that he had no signal. He'd have to hoof it into town and hope they had a repair place. He could handle minor repairs but, unless he missed his guess, he was looking at something major. He grabbed a bottle of water from the cooler, slung his leather jacket over his shoulder, locked the truck, and headed down the highway.

A stiff breeze took the edge off the hot summer day, but almost immediately, sweat began dripping down his face, only to evaporate in the dry desert air. He dribbled some water on the back of his neck and tried to focus on the landscape.

The golden sun hung high overhead in a cornflower blue sky, shining down on a rolling landscape of juniper, cactus, yucca, and a whole lot of dirt and rock. In the distance, two russet-colored buttes stood out in sharp contrast to the dull brown earth. Because he had nothing else to do, he focused on the hill on the left and tried to estimate its height, then calculated how long it would take him to free-climb the steepest side.

He'd just about completed his estimate when he heard the sound of a vehicle coming up behind him, and turned to see a battered red Honda Accord coming his way. He didn't bother putting out his thumb. Few strangers were comfortable giving a ride to a long-haired, six foot five Native American.

The Accord slowed to a stop alongside him and the driver called out to him. "That your truck back there?"

Bones nodded as he looked the girl up and down. She was Latina with rich caramel skin, full lips, and glossy black hair that hung halfway down her back. She wore a pink midriff tank top, tight-fitting blue jeans, and big sunglasses.

"Yep. That's me."

"Out of gas? In this part of the country you've got to fill up every chance you get. Service stations are few and far between."

"I wish. It's something mechanical for sure."

"Sorry to hear that. Hop in and I'll give you a ride."

Bones heard the passenger door unlock, and he slipped inside. The air conditioning was running at full blast but produced little in the way of cool air. It was in dire need of juicing up, but from the looks of the girl's battered vehicle, he doubted she had the money for such a luxury.

"I'm Marisol. Mari for short." She held out her hand to shake, and he found her grip surprisingly strong.

"Bones. And don't bother asking my birth name, because I won't tell you."

"Fair enough." She glanced in the rear-view mirror and guided the Honda back onto the empty highway. "We don't see many natives off the reservation out here, but you're clearly not from around here. I saw your Florida license plate. Seminole?"

"Cherokee. Originally from North Carolina, but I've lived in the Keys since I left the Navy."

Mari sighed. "I've never seen the ocean. My parents were supposed to take me to Disney once when I was a kid, but my dad got drunk and wrecked our car." She shrugged as if to say, 'What are you gonna do?'

Bones managed a half-smile. "Saw plenty of that growing up. The stereotype about Indians and fire water isn't entirely undeserved."

"How about you? Do you drink?"

"I wouldn't say no to a cold one, but it's a little early in the day for a drink. How about tonight?" He glanced at the ring finger of her left hand, saw it empty, and flashed his most roguish grin in her direction.

Panic flashed across Mari's face. "Oh, I didn't mean that. I work at a bar and grill in town. The only one of either, in fact." She turned and stared into the side-view mirror. "I just thought you might like to drop in after you get your truck taken care of."

As she turned her head, Bones caught a glimpse of a

bruise over her right eye. So the big sunglasses weren't solely for the purpose of keeping down the glare.

"It's cool," he said. "I've got an idea. How about, after your shift is over, I buy you a drink. Maybe whoever gave you that shiner will be stupid enough to show up and say something about it."

Mari jerked her head around, and the car swerved into the emergency lane. She overcorrected in the other direction, and Bones snatched the wheel with one hand and guided them back on course.

"I'm so sorry," she said. "I'm just really out of it today. I got this," she gestured at her eye, "rock climbing. Had a bit of a fall."

"So you don't have a boyfriend?"

"Yeah, I do."

"Is he the one who took you rock climbing?"

Mari grimaced, her jaw working for a few seconds. "The repair shop is right up there."

She nodded at a metal building with a large open bay on the front. A sun-bleached mural of hot air balloons floating across a desert landscape adorned the near side.

"Balloon Fiesta," Mari said. "They do it in Albuquerque every year. You should check it out."

"Sounds like something white people would do." Bones said, eliciting a giggle from Mari. "I might check it out if the beer is cold and the women are hot."

"So you like old, white women?" Mari teased, clearly relieved that the subject had moved away from her bruised eye.

"I just like women."

Mari pulled into the parking lot of Miguel's Automotive and Pawn. Rather, she drove off the road and onto the flat patch of dirt in front of the building, brought the car to a stop, but left the engine running. "Here's where I leave you."

"Thanks for the ride." Bones squeezed his large frame out of the Honda. He immediately felt the heat of the sun on his black hair and wondered if Manny's had air conditioning. "Where do I go if I want to get that drink later?"

"Down there on the left. It's part of the motor lodge. If you're stuck here overnight, that's the only place to stay in town."

In a different set of circumstances, Bones would have asked if she had room at her place, but the girl's situation was clearly complicated. A part of him wanted to do something about it, but he'd been in such situations before and knew how little difference his style of intervention truly made.

"All right. I might see you later."

Mari wiggled her fingers in a dainty sort of wave and drove away.

Bones managed a grin and then turned and headed for the front door of the repair shop. A sign in the dust-coated window read, "We Sell Green Chile." He pushed the door open and stuck his head inside. A glass-topped counter filled with knives, pistols, and turquoise jewelry ran across the room. Behind it, shelves piled with old DVDs, video games, and various odds and ends lined the back wall. In the corner, a gun case coated in cobwebs held a few shotguns and a single Glock.

"Lots of crap for sale, but no one to do the selling," he muttered. "Hello?" he called.

No reply.

He waited for a count of twenty before calling out again, louder this time. "Yo! Anybody here like money, because I need to spend some."

A toilet flushed somewhere behind the bookshelf. A few seconds later, a portion of shelf swung forward, and a graying man with dark brown skin and light brown teeth grinned his way into the shop.

"No need to rush me, bro. In New Mexico, we all operate on Indian time." His face went slack. "Whoa! No offense, big man."

"It's cool. My grandfather says the same thing about the reservation where I grew up. Are you Miguel?"

The man frowned and then cackled with laughter. "No way, bro. Miguel was my grandfather. I'm Manny."

"I'm Bones." They shook hands. Manny's firm, calloused grip told the tale of years of manual labor.

"You're going to stand out around here. There's only two kinds of people in Quemadura: Mexicans and Mixicans."

Bones frowned. "What's a Mixican?"

"Mexican mixed with something else." Manny cackled. "Except for the cactus, juniper, and chile, everything here is some shade of brown."

Bones decided he liked the old man in spite of his annoying laugh.

"So, what brings you in today? I don't imagine you drove here just to check out my knife collection." He tapped the glass counter with a gnarled finger, the grease under the nail forming a black crescent moon.

"Truck broke down." Bones described the problem and gave the make and model of his truck.

Manny clucked his tongue. "Should have bought a Ford."

"I'll debate you on that all day long. It's ten years old, and I've never had a problem. Until now," he added.

"Consuela's thirty years old, and she's been nothing but problems, but she still runs. Come on. We'll get your truck."

Consuela was a battered Ford pickup whose brown paint blended seamlessly into the landscape. Manny kept up a steady stream of chatter about the menu at the Blue Corn Grill where Mari worked. He recommended the cheese quesadilla, primarily because he had his doubts about the meat served up at the town's only diner.

"You ever see a roof rat? Grande! Everybody's got them. My place has got them. The motor court's got them. But Blue Corn? No roof rats. Think about that. Where do they go?"

"Into the burritos?" Bones guessed.

"Bingo."

Bones vowed to stick to beer and chips until he got back onto the road.

Half an hour later, after towing Bones' truck back to the shop and giving it a quick inspection, Manny delivered the news Bones had feared.

"You dropped your tranny, bro."

Under a different set of circumstances, he would have turned that phrase into a perverse joke, but when it meant he had to pony up the cash for a new transmission, humor was in short supply. There went most of what he'd planned on spending in Vegas.

"How soon can you have it ready?"

Manny considered the question. "I can get the parts day after tomorrow. I can have the work done the next day, assuming my nephew's sober enough to help me."

Bones resisted the urge to roll his eyes. This was, after all, the smallest of small towns. "Looks like I'll be hanging around town for a few days. Any suggestions on how to kill time?"

Manny shrugged. "I think the motor inn has HBO."

Bones gathered his belongings, thanked Manny for his help, and headed off down the road toward the motor inn. The heat rising up from the asphalt shimmered, giving the town a slightly out of focus quality. One hour ago he'd been on his way to Sin City to reconnect with an old flame. Now he was facing three days of zero kicks on Route 66. Sometimes life sucked.

TWO

The Blue Corn Grill smelled of burger grease, roasted chile, and stale beer. The afternoon sun shone through the dusty windows, casting dull beams on the warped wooden floor, stained by the spills of decades of tipsy clients. Three men in work uniforms sat around a table, loudly debating the relative merits of the Dallas Cowboys and Denver Broncos. When Bones walked in, they all gave him a quick glance. He raised his chin by way of greeting. The men returned the gesture, looking like baby ducks waiting to be fed, and then went back to their conversation. Mariachi music blared from an old jukebox. Bones smiled. Swap out the mariachi for some Metallica and he'd be right at home.

Marisol stood with her back to the bar, filling a pitcher with beer. Bones propped his elbows on the bar and waited for her to turn around.

"Oh my God, you scared me," she said when her eyes fell on him. "What are you doing, stalker?"

"I didn't want to interrupt you when you're hard at work."

She rolled her eyes. "I've got three customers. Four if I count you."

"Why wouldn't you count me? I'm awesome, and I'm a good tipper."

She laughed at that. "We'll see. Did you get checked into the motor lodge all right?"

"Sure did. Surprisingly, they had a ton of rooms available. I guess it isn't tourist season."

"It hasn't been tourist season for as long as this town has been here. Hold on a minute."

Bones waited while she carried the pitcher of beer over to the table where the football fans were still arguing. Embroiled in a heated Tony Romo versus Peyton Manning dispute, they hardly noticed her.

"So," she said, wiping her hands on her jeans, "what will you have?"

"How are the chicken fingers?" Bones asked, scanning the chalkboard behind the bar where the menu was written in a delicate, feminine hand.

"Frozen. Same as the burger patties. The hot dogs are awful. The locals usually go for the burrito or the huevos rancheros."

Remembering what Manny had said about the burritos, Bones decided on the latter. "Huevos rancheros sounds good. Eggs over easy, if you don't mind."

Mari nodded. "Red or green?"

"What?"

"I forgot you're not from around here," she said. "Everything comes with chile on it. Do you want red or green?"

"Can I have both?"

"Christmas tree it is. What to drink?"

"Tell me you have Dos Equis with a lime. After the day I've had, I need one. Maybe more than one."

"Dos Equis I have. No limes."

"Good enough." Bones accepted the ice cold bottle, chose a table close to the bar, and took a seat. He rocked back, stretching his long legs out, and gazed out the window. There wasn't much to see outside, but Mari was the only thing worth looking at in here, and he wasn't the kind to stare. He thought about his friends, Willis and Matt, arriving in Vegas tomorrow without him. Twenty-four hours from now, they'd be living it up, surrounded by bright lights and beautiful women, while Bones would be here, surrounded by juniper. Not much of a tradeoff.

A few minutes later, Mari slid a plate onto the table. Bones' mouth watered at the sight of the heaping pile of pinto beans, cheese, and green chile over two blue corn tortillas and topped with three eggs and served with a side of fried potatoes. You couldn't get this at a Vegas buffet. He was just digging in when she sat another, identical dish on his table along with a steaming cup of coffee.

"I know I'm a big dude, but I can't eat that much. At least, not if I want to keep my girlish figure."

"It's for Manny." She giggled and playfully punched him on the shoulder. "He comes in at the same time every day and orders the same thing. I like to have it ready for him." She glanced up. "See? Here he is."

Manny bounded into the restaurant, greeted the customers with a wave and a loud "Ola!" and then took at seat across from Bones. "You saved me a seat." Without further word, he dug into his meal.

The two men ate in companionable silence. When they'd both cleared their plates, they enjoyed their drinks and made small talk. Manny was an army veteran and had a few tales to tell. Every one of them involved women and alcohol, not necessarily in that order. Bones was beginning to feel right at home when a new customer entered.

He was a tall, sturdily-built Anglo of about an age with Bones. He wore his sandy-blond hair cut short, and his beard and mustache were neatly trimmed. Despite the heat, he was dressed in khaki pants and a long-sleeved blue Oxford cloth shirt. As he passed the table where the football talk had finally subsided, he greeted the three patrons in an overly loud voice.

"Wish I could join you for a drink," he said, "but I've got this book to finish." He held up a laptop case and grinned. He turned and headed for the bar, the men at the table rolling their eyes and shaking their head as he walked away.

"That's Matthew." Manny looked like he'd sucked a lemon.

"What's his deal? He's friendly to the other guys in here, but he blows you off?"

Manny cackled. "That's because I think he's full of mierda de toro, and he knows it."

"That means 'bullcrap,' right?"

"A little less delicate, but you got the general idea." Manny took a sip of coffee.

"So, what's his story?" Bones asked as he watched Matthew open his laptop, turn it on, slip on a pair of reading glasses, and then look around to see if anyone was watching. "He's a writer, I take it."

"Not really. He's a schoolteacher in the next town over but wants everyone to think he's a big-time writer. Claims he's working on 'something huge'." Manny waggled his fingers as he said the last. "He's published a few books, but I think only his mom has read them."

Bones chuckled. "This seems like a weird place to work on a book."

"For him, it's more about the image than it is about actually succeeding. He's here for two reasons: to get attention, and to keep an eye on Mari."

Bones shifted in his seat. "Is that her boyfriend?"

Manny nodded. "I don't know what she sees in him. She's a good girl, and smart, too. She went to college for a couple of years but came back when her Abuela got cancer. After the old lady died, the life just went out of Mari. She took a job here and hasn't left since."

A cacophony of conflicting thoughts ran through Bones' mind. Odds were, Matthew was the one who had given Mari that shiner. Bones' inclination was to drag the guy out back and introduce him to Bones' fist. But he didn't know for sure that Matthew was the culprit, and if Bones landed himself in jail, he'd definitely miss out on Vegas.

Manny seemed to read his thoughts. "There's not much anyone can do for her until she's ready to stand up for herself," he said. "Believe me, we keep trying. Nobody's giving up on her."

Bones nodded. Up at the bar, Mari and Matthew were engaged in a heated discussion. Matthew jerked his head to the side and glared at Bones, who responded with a wink.

"Oh no, Boss, why did you do that?" Manny whispered. "Now he's going to come over here, and homie wears way too much cologne."

Manny was correct on both accounts. Back ramrod-straight, chest puffed out, and elbows slightly cocked, Matthew stalked over to their table, a sickly-sweet cloud of musk preceding his arrival by almost a full second.

"You got a problem, mister?" Matthew asked.

"I got a whole list of them," Bones said. "Starting with an asshat who's interrupting me while I'm trying to enjoy my beer. Think you can help me with that?" He grinned at Matthew, who was clearly sizing him up.

Finally, the man's lips drew back in a mirthless smile. "You're a funny guy. I'll have to write you into a book sometime." He stood there for a full three seconds before returning to his seat at the bar.

"You hurt his feelings," Manny said in a low voice. "He wanted you to ask him about his book. You know, treat him like a bestselling author, like that Harry Potter guy."

Bones didn't bother to correct Manny. He gulped down the last of his beer and held up the empty bottle to signal Mari that he'd like another.

"So, what does he write about?"

"He wrote some weird science fiction stuff, but now he says he's doing some serious investigative work, and that when he's finished, everybody will be blown away by what he's discovered." Manny smirked.

"Any idea what he's working on?"

"Rumor has it," Manny said, leaning forward, "he's been asking questions about aliens."

THREE

Bones slowed from a jog to a walk as the rocky hills came into view. The orange ball of the late afternoon sun hung low on the western horizon. Colored the same dirty, reddish-brown as the rest of the landscape, the hills cast long shadows across the cactus-dotted landscape. It would have made a nice painting if he was into that sort of thing.

Having nothing better to do, Bones had gone for a run with this dark spot on the horizon as his target. The hills had looked taller from a distance, and he had hoped maybe they would offer some decent climbing, but up close they weren't all that impressive. It was only the flat lie of the surrounding land that lent this place the illusion of height.

When he reached the base of the closest hill, he stopped and took a swig of water. Tepid as it was, it was still refreshing in this dry climate. He probably should have brought more than a liter, but he hadn't planned on running this far. Not for the first time he wondered how the hell he was going to kill time out here in this empty patch of dirt.

He took a moment to walk along the base of the hills, examining them with casual disinterest. Though none of them were more than eighty feet tall, the edges were steep. Wind and perhaps a little bit of rain had scoured their surfaces clean, leaving bare stone with only the occasional clump of weeds stubbornly clinging to its surface like patches of beard missed during a hurried shave.

He soon came upon a heap of tumbled down rock. A quick inspection told him that changes in temperature had caused the rocky hills above to crack and large portions to shear off. Here the face was almost perpendicular in spots.

"Looks like a good place for a free climb." He took another swallow of water, capped the bottle, and stowed it in the shade under some loose rocks. He would want the rest of it for his trek back to town.

He took a minute to choose his way up. What he was about to do was foolish, he knew. Free climbing was dangerous and to do it without a partner even more so. But, Bones was reckless even at the best of times. Boredom tended to turn it up a notch or three.

When he was finally satisfied that he had selected a route that was sufficiently challenging but unlikely to kill him, he began his ascent. It felt good to work muscles that had gone largely unused since he'd begun his cross-country drive. He wasn't one for sitting around for very long, and his body seemed to be chastising him for a couple of sedentary days. Twinges of pain danced across his back and shoulders as he made his way upward. Higher and higher he climbed, his fingers and the toes of his shoes picking out every crack and crevice. Spiderlike, he clambered up the first fifty feet before he hit a dead end. That was all right; it only added to the challenge.

He backtracked a few feet, mentally plotted a new route, and moved to his left until he could resume his ascent. He was almost at the top when things got ugly.

At that moment, one toehold and one handhold chose to give way simultaneously. He cursed as he felt himself slipping down the hill. He held on tight with one hand, his fingers digging into the split rock. His shoulder wrenched and hot pain burned along the length of his arm. If he had torn his rotator cuff, he was going to be pissed.

"Look on the bright side," he grumbled. "At least no one's around to see you dangling here like a…"

The roar of an engine and the crunch of tires on rocky ground made a liar of him. He steadied himself, finding new hand and footholds, and looked back to see who was coming. A battered Jeep drew a dusty line across the parched earth as it approached. Figuring he didn't have any friends in this neck of the woods, and knowing this was public land, and therefore he couldn't be trespassing on anyone's private property, he turned and resumed his climb.

The rumble of the Jeep grew louder, bringing with it the twang of country music. Bones closed his eyes and winced.

"Don't be a redneck. Please don't be a redneck."

Down below, the Jeep scraped to a halt, the music dying as the engine choked into silence. A door slammed shut.

"What are you doing up there?" The voice was male and slightly high-pitched, with a light touch of accent on the o's that was typical of so many New Mexicans.

"Performance art," Bones called down without looking. "I accept tips. Just put them under a rock so they don't blow away."

"You need to come down from there." The speaker sounded uncertain.

"It's cool. I've done this before. Now, why don't you leave me alone before you make me fall?" Bones was about ten feet short of the summit. Here, the rock face angled outward a few degrees, making for a challenging finish.

"I'm a sheriff's deputy, and I'm telling you to come down from there right now."

Bones finally looked down. The man was a thickset Latino dressed in blue jeans, cowboy boots, and a checked shirt. His left hand rested on an automatic pistol holstered on his hip.

"If you really are a deputy, that means you're not a Fed and this is BLM land."

The deputy grunted a mirthless laugh. "That will probably hold up in court," he admitted. "Of course, you might sit in jail for a long time before you come to trial. We're really slow with paperwork."

Bones took a deep breath and let it out slowly. "I'm climbing a freaking hill on public land. Why do you care?"

"It's for your own safety."

"In that case, it's probably better if I climb these last few feet to the top instead of coming all the way back down. I'll chill out up here, and you can send a chopper to pick me up."

The deputy ignored that. "I could just shoot you, but you don't want that, do you? I've already called the sheriff," he added.

That sealed it. It was all a big pile of crap, but Bones didn't need the hassle. Who the hell knew what small town justice looked like around here? "All right. I'm coming down."

He took his sweet time, not because he feared falling, but because he wanted to make the deputy, if that's really what the guy was, wait as long as possible. When he finally reached the ground, he took a moment to brush himself off and wipe his bloody fingertips on the sandy ground before turning around.

At about five-eight, the deputy stood nearly a foot shorter than Bones, and he took an involuntary step backward as the big Cherokee approached him.

"How did you get here?" the deputy asked.

"Aliens dropped me off in their spaceship."

He flinched at that, probably not accustomed to being spoken to in this way. He squeezed the grip of his pistol and then released it. "You got a car around here or motorcycle or something?"

Bones shook his head.

The deputy waited, but he got no more of a response. Bones had plenty of time to kill until his truck was ready, and spending it making this idiot miserable was at least better entertainment than staring at the walls of his motel room. Let the man stew in his own juices for a while. He could do this all day.

"Tell you what," the deputy finally said. "Leave now and we'll forget this ever happened. I'll tell the sheriff you cooperated. Like I said, it's just about safety."

Bones looked up at the sky, pretending to consider the deputy's words. Finally, he nodded once. "Whatever, dude." He retrieved his water bottle, took a drink, mostly to make the deputy wait a little longer, and headed back toward town.

As he strode past the Jeep, he noticed for the first time someone sitting in the passenger seat. It was Matthew, wannabe author, and Mari's boyfriend. He inclined his head and pointed at Matthew to let him know he'd been spotted.

"Now that," he said to himself as he turned away, "is interesting."

FOUR

The knock at the door came again, harder this time. Bones turned off the shower, grabbed a towel, and opened the bathroom door.

"Hold on a minute!" He pushed his long hair back out of his face, wrapped the towel around his waist and, still dripping, headed to the door. A thin trail of water followed him across the threadbare carpet. When he got to the door, he peered out through the security peephole and smiled.

Marisol stood there, gazing intently at the door as if she could see right through it.

"This is a surprise," he said as he unlocked the door and opened it. "Come on in."

"This isn't a social call. I just…" Her eyes widened when she saw his state of undress. "Do you always answer the door naked?"

"Only when somebody keeps pounding on the door when I'm trying to shower. Besides, I'm not naked. I'm wearing a towel."

"That's a hand towel." She pointedly looked the other way.

Bones looked down and realized that, in his hurry, he had indeed grabbed a towel that barely covered his hips and pelvis. "First peek is free. Anything more than that you've got to buy me dinner."

"Could you just get dressed? I'm in a hurry." Mari turned her back on him and stood, arms crossed, tapping her foot while he pulled on shorts and a t-shirt.

"You don't mind if I go commando, do you?"

She let out an exasperated sigh. Even that was cute, Bones noticed. "Oh my God," she said, "are you always like this?"

"Give me time. I only get better." He dropped down on the corner of the bed, eliciting a strained squeal from the aging box springs. "You can turn around now. I'm as decent as I ever get."

Mari took a quick glance back to make sure he was, in fact, dressed, before she turned all the way around.

"What were you doing out at Halcón Rock?" she asked without preamble.

"Oh, is that what it's called?"

"Just tell me." She took a deep breath and bit her lip. "Please?"

"It's cool. I'm into climbing. I went for a run, saw the, what did you call it, Halcón Rock, and thought I'd give it a go."

"Just like that? You saw a rock and decided to scale it?"

"That's sort of how rock climbing works. Do you climb?"

Mari shook her head. "Matthew thinks," she hesitated, "that you went out there just to mess with him."

"That would be a trick since I didn't know anyone was going to be out there. I might be devilishly handsome and wickedly charming, but I'm not psychic."

Mari considered this for a quiet moment. "And of all places, you just happened to wander out there?"

"Dude, I've never been here before. I went for a run to kill time, and that's where I ended up. What's so special about that place?"

"Nothing," she said, much too fast. "It's just that Matthew was out there, and I was afraid you might have gone out there to start something with him."

"Why would I do that?" Bones knew the answer, and he suspected she did too, but he wanted to hear her say it.

"No reason, really. It's just that he sometimes rubs people the wrong way. I saw you two talking earlier, and I thought maybe you might have, I don't know, taken a dislike to him."

"I hated that idiot before I even met him, and you know why."

Mari hung her head.

He softened his tone. "Why do you put up with him? You're awesome, and he's a tool."

Mari giggled at that. "You don't know me at all. I'm not that great."

Bones rose and, in two steps, closed the distance between them. He reached out to brush the hair back from her bruised eye, but she flinched and took a step backward.

"Sorry," he said. "Listen, I know relationships are complicated, but this is the simplest thing in the world. You need to get away from this guy for your own safety. Hell, get out of this town. If you need my help, I'm here. Whatever it takes." Mari was right; he didn't know her. But he couldn't stand to see a person stuck in a situation like hers. He had to at least offer.

"Thank you," she whispered. "But you don't know what you're offering. Matthew's dangerous, and it's not just him."

"I promise you, I've faced a million times worse." He almost laughed. Mari wouldn't believe half of the things he'd done in his life.

"I should go," she said, taking another step back. "It's a small town, and someone might notice me hanging around here."

"Let them talk. Maybe your boyfriend would be stupid enough to make an issue of it."

Mari shook her head. "Will you just promise me you'll stay away from Halcón Rock?"

"I will if you'll tell me why."

A curtain seemed to draw down over her eyes. That request was obviously a non-starter. She cocked her head and frowned. "Did you really run all the way out there and then climb the rock?"

"Almost. I still had about ten feet to go when Deputy Dipshit and your fellow showed up."

Mari smiled. "Deputy Dipshit. I'll have to remember that one." She fell silent. They stood, gazing at one another, Mari not crossing the threshold, but not making a move to leave, either. "Is this what they call an uncomfortable silence?"

"I'm not uncomfortable, but I think you'd be a lot more comfortable if you came inside and closed the door. We can just talk."

She twitched, as if she were about to take a step toward him, but froze. "You have a lot of scars. I peeked a little bit."

"I was a Navy SEAL. I've been through some stuff."

"I'll bet you've got some stories to tell." The eye contact was gone.

"Plenty. Want to hear a few?"

"Yeah," she said. "Maybe tomorrow at lunchtime." She turned and hurried away without a goodbye.

Bones moved to the doorway and watched her walk to her car, get in, and drive away. When she was gone, he closed the door, grabbed his cell phone, and did a quick search for Halcón Rock. The results made him whistle.

"Holy crap. I think I need to go back for another look."

FIVE

No one was about when Bones slipped out of his motel room and headed down the street. He kept to the darkest shadows, which wasn't difficult since there were no streetlights—at least, none that worked. The dim glow of the neon light in window of the Blue Corn Grill cast a pool of light on the ground, and Bones found himself longing for the cool, blue waters of the Gulf of Mexico. That or the giant swimming pool at Mandalay Bay. He wasn't particular.

High above, a dusting of stars twinkled in the clear night sky. The dim, glowing band of the Milky Way galaxy lay just above the horizon. Quemadura might be a hole in the wall, but the night sky was spectacular. You didn't see skies like this back east. Humming the Eagles' song, "Peaceful, Easy Feeling," Bones crossed the street and struck out across the open desert.

When he was well clear of town, he turned on his phone and started reading one of the articles he had found on Halcón Rock. It was a piece from the *Santa Fe Sun*. He did a double-take when he saw the name of the author of the piece.

"Amanda Shores. What are the odds?" Smiling at pleasant memories, he began to read.

SUBTERRANEAN SLAUGHTER?

For more than a half-century, New Mexico and aliens have gone hand-in-hand in the national consciousness. From stories of battles at secret alien bases to perhaps the most notorious story of them all, the Roswell Incident, when someone thinks of aliens, their thoughts almost always turn to New Mexico.

Roswell, New Mexico has, understandably, received the most attention in this regard. From the well-known museum to the space-themed cafes, all the way down to the streetlamps shaped like the heads of visitors from beyond, the city had cultivated the alien connection and parlayed it into a modest but respectable tourist trade, drawing both the casual visitor and the dedicated researcher. Roswell, however, is far from the first community in this state to be associated with alien contact.

While so-called UFO experts focus their attentions on the most recent and renowned stories, reports of alien contact in the region date back to the indigenous peoples who made their homes here long before contact with European explorers. Reports of strange lights in the sky, artistic representations of strange beings and crafts, and even direct contact with extraterrestrials are common to the lore of tribes of the Southwest and beyond.

One such story survives in Apache lore. According to the legend, a group of warriors were descended upon during the night by a handful of alien-looking beings. The men were short, with lean, gray bodies and bulbous heads and carried "flashing spears full of fire."

Though Apache are widely regarded as the finest warriors among the Southwestern tribes, masters of camouflage and ambush, the dozen or more warriors were helpless against the handful of strange beings. Only two of the original party managed to escape.

While most people would consider this nothing more than a story, one elder claims to have in his possession proof of the encounter. According to his account, one surviving warrior fought hand-to-hand with one of the attackers, managed to wound it with his knife, and came away holding something that belonged to the strange visitor. This artifact has allegedly been handed down for hundreds of years and has never been shown to the public. Whether it exists at all, who can say?

An interesting wrinkle to the story of this incident, which allegedly took place at the foot of Halcón Rock near Quemadura, is that the aliens came, not from the sky, but up from beneath the earth. The Apache saw neither lights in the sky nor strange crafts of any kind. Depending on which version of the story one believes, the aliens either descended from the top of the rock formation or came up from somewhere underneath it.

Few, if any, researchers have investigated the story. Those who have tried report being turned away by members of the local Sheriff's Department. A Santa Fe Sun reporter received similar treatment when attempting to visit Halcón Rock, despite the monument's location on public land. The deputy at the scene cited safety concerns, but otherwise declined to comment.

Quemadura-based author and self-described UFO skeptic Matthew Jameson dismissed the legend as mere fancy.

"The locals don't take the story seriously," said Jameson. "I promise you; no one has seen any aliens wandering around here. Spreading this sort of story is nothing more than an excuse to set up a t-shirt stand. We'll leave that to our friends in Roswell."

Did aliens once live beneath the red rocks of eastern New Mexico?

Do they live there still? Perhaps we'll never know.

Bones closed the browser window and turned off his phone to preserve the battery. There wasn't much there to go on, but Matthew Jameson was obviously the same Matthew he'd encountered earlier. Mari's boyfriend. The man had some sort of interest in Halcón Rock, and if Bones didn't miss his guess, the man believed there was something there, and Matthew wanted to be the first to find it. Add in the fact that the local authorities consistently patrolled and chased away visitors from a location that wasn't strictly theirs to control access to, and the whole thing stank like a men's locker room.

Eager to see what he could find, Bones set out a steady jog. Soon, the dark shape of the rock formation loomed against the starlit horizon. Bones grinned. This time, he would make it to the top and see what Matthew was hiding up there.

SIX

Aside from the view, the top of Halcón Rock had little to recommend it. Rocky spikes and spikier clumps of yucca dotted the flat top of the rock formation. To the south, a few faint lights marked Quemadura where it dozed beneath the starry sky. He took a moment to savor the cool, late-night desert breeze that swept over him, letting it reinvigorate his tired body. After a few minutes soaking up the tranquility, he was ready to search.

"All right, Matthew, let's see what big secret you're hiding up here." He made a circuit of the top of the rock, relying on his keen night vision. No sense breaking out his Maglite and possibly drawing attention to himself unless absolutely necessary. He picked his way carefully along the uneven surface, keeping an eye out for anything unusual.

His turn around the rock took about twenty minutes, and nothing leaped out at him. He supposed it was possible that it wasn't the top of the rock per se, but the rock in general that Matthew and the deputy were keeping outsiders clear of. After all, the article had said the so-called aliens might have come up from underground. But, he had gone to the trouble of climbing up here so he might as well make a thorough inspection.

He took out his Maglite and replaced the clear lens with a red one, which would better preserve his night vision and be harder to spot from a distance. Cupping the flashlight to hide the beam, he began working a grid back across the rock. Maddock, his best friend and business partner, would be proud of him. Whenever they searched for a sunken ship, Maddock preferred the orderly, painstaking approach to searches while Bones would prefer to wing it. In fairness, winging it didn't often work out, but when it did, it saved them a great deal of time and spared Bones a wealth of boredom.

This search proved equally fruitless. Ten yards away, a tall stone spire marked the west end of the rock, with nothing but coarse stone to fill the intervening space.

"I guess it's back down again. At least I got to do some more climbing." More out of a sense of obligation than purpose he completed his search. When he reached the spire, he let out a whistle. "What have we got here?"

Footprints scuffed the sunbaked patch of dirt at the foot of the spire, and off to the side lay a deep scrape where something heavy had been dragged a short distance. Someone had been busy in this very spot.

A manhole-sized slab of rock lay at an angle against the base of the spire. Bones heaved against it and slid it to the side.

"Jackpot!" A dark shaft dropped down about five feet to a narrow passageway that disappeared into the darkness. By the looks of it, it was just wide enough to accommodate his bulk. "Dark, creepy tunnel heading down into who knows where? This is totally my jam." Heart racing, he slid feet-first into the passageway.

Once inside, he exchanged his red lens for the standard clear one. Down here his night vision would be useless, and there was no danger of anyone seeing him so he might as well have as much light as possible.

The way down was steep and irregular, a natural fissure exacerbated over time by the heating and cooling of the rock and washed clean by occasional rainfalls. He slipped, slid, and clambered deeper into the darkness until he finally came down in a low chamber about twenty feet across. He shone his light all around. A few stalactites dangled from the ceiling and white cave pearls glinted on the floor. Multiple passageways led off in various directions. He'd found his way into a cavern system.

"Holy crap. I don't have time to explore every freaking one of these."

He didn't have to explore at all. A quick inspection revealed that someone, Matthew, he assumed, had marked all but one of the openings with an X in yellow chalk.

"I wonder how long it took him to explore and eliminate all these other passageways." Grinning at the thought of benefitting from what likely represented months, if not years, of Matthew's efforts, Bones headed down the unmarked passageway.

Like most caverns, the way twisted and turned, rose and fell, but gradually descended. He lost all sense of how far he'd traveled in this dark, unrelenting stone tube. He kept a sure grip on his Maglite, knowing he'd be in trouble if he should lose it.

After traveling for a good fifteen minutes, bypassing several caves and passages marked with an X, he came to a halt at the edge of a yawning pit. Smooth-sided and twenty feet across, it dropped fifty feet or more to a rock-choked bottom. The passageway continued on the other side.

Bones shone his light around, and the beam fell on a pile of lumber, all short lengths of two-by-fours, a box of nails, and a hammer. He chuckled. Was Matthew going to try and build a bridge out of three-foot long boards?

"I'll bet that idiot tried to carry standard length lumber down here and couldn't make it through the tight curves. Wish I'd been there to see it." Smiling, he played his light around the cavern, wondering how he might make it across. One option was to climb down into the pit and then climb back up the other side, but he'd need gear and a partner for that. Perhaps there was another way.

He carefully inspected the chamber and realized that the walls weren't smooth at all. Deep, jagged clefts split the surface, running horizontally from one side of the defile to the other. A spark of an idea kindled his adventurous spirit. His friends called it "reckless" but Bones knew his capabilities.

"I can do this." His eyes followed the flashlight beam as it dropped to the bottom of the pit far below. "I'd better do this or else I'm screwed."

He took a minute to try and talk himself out of this course of action. There was no need, he thought, to investigate any further. What did he care if Matthew was looking for underworld aliens? It wasn't his problem. Why risk falling, maybe to his death, just to beat the man to the other side?

But the truth was, this wasn't about besting Matthew. This was about Bones' innate curiosity and his fascination with all things strange and mysterious. It was the sort of legend he and Maddock were always chasing down, and usually doing it in much more perilous circumstances than this. Bones wasn't a fearful man, and he wasn't about to be deterred by a challenging climb.

His mind now made up, he took time to plan his route. He wished he had a helmet lamp, and helmet to put it on, but his Maglite would have to do. His eyes traced the cracks in the rock, picking out handholds and footholds. When he was satisfied he'd chosen the best path, he clamped his flashlight in his teeth, slid his foot into a crevasse, and began to climb.

SEVEN

Bones worked his way across the chasm, his thoughts focused on nothing but the next handhold or foothold. In the deep recesses of his mind he was aware of the precipitous fall that would result from a single mistake, but if he did what he was supposed to do, it wouldn't matter. All he had to do was remain focused on the task at hand.

Adrenaline coursed through him, all his senses alive. What was it about putting himself in mortal peril that excited him so? It was just the way he was wired, and that wasn't going to change. Plenty of people had tried to break him of it, and all had failed.

When he stepped onto solid ground again, he took a moment to look back at the way he'd come, making a mental note of the path he'd taken so he could reverse it on the way back. Finally satisfied he had it down, he hurried along the passageway.

He rounded a sharp turn and stopped short. Twenty paces ahead, beyond a floor strewn with debris, and set in a wall covered in pictographs, a gleaming metal door barred the way. He saw no hinge or doorframe. It was as if the metal was part of the wall. He took a few steps closer, running his light up and down its length. It was flawless. Not a single scratch or spot of rust marred its surface.

"What the hell is this made of?" he muttered. "Titanium?" He moved closer, picking his way through the debris that he now recognized as signs of sacrifice—shriveled ears of corn, dried flowers twisted into wreaths, fetishes crafted from sticks and yucca fibers, and the bones of small animals. Sometime, most likely in the distant past, the native peoples had known of this place and had apparently sought to appease whoever, or whatever lived behind the door.

Bones extended a hand to touch the door but hesitated. Should he touch it? What if it was electrified or something? He reached out and tapped the door with his Maglite. Nothing. The door seemed to absorb sound. He repeated the procedure with the blade of his knife. Still nothing.

"Oh, what the hell? You didn't come all this way to wuss out now." He took a deep breath and pressed his palm to the surface of the door. The icy cold metal grew warm at his touch and then went cold again. "That's it?" He tried it with his other hand. Same result.

Disappointed, he banged on the door a few times, then tried pushing it, but to no avail. He looked for a handle, a controller, or even a seam around the edges, but even up close it looked to be a part of the natural rock. He could no longer keep the thoughts of aliens out of his mind. All the stories he'd ever read about extraterrestrials in New Mexico began to scroll through his mind. Could this be proof? It was certainly something, but it wouldn't mean much if he couldn't get to the other side.

He took a few steps back and shone his light over the cave walls, inspecting the pictographs. Many were common sights to the Southwest: spirals, suns, and animals, but he saw several variations on the same theme—people bowing down to starry-eyed men who were climbing up long staircases.

"Well, they aren't coming down from the sky, that's for sure." He took out his phone and snapped pictures of the cavern, recording the door and all the surrounding pictographs in as much detail as he could. He gave the door one more try to see if it would budge, but again he felt only the brief flash of warmth as if the door were trying to recognize him. Finally, he accepted there was nothing more he could do at the moment. He'd go back to the motel, get some sleep, and make a plan on how to further investigate. He could think of worse ways to kill a few days.

The climb back over the chasm took a little longer than it had on the way in. No longer buoyed by the thrill of anticipation, he slogged across, trying not to let his thoughts drift to what lay beyond the door. Once he missed a step and let out a curse as he held on tight, his toe searching to rediscover its hold. Just as he found it, he heard a low, muffled sound drifting through the cavern. An echo of his cry?

And then he heard it again. The sound of voices.

Someone was coming.

"That's going to be Matthew. Crap." He completed the climb across, hurried over to the pile of building materials where he ducked down to listen. The voices were still indistinct but coming closer. He could tell there were two different speakers. Perhaps Matthew and the deputy?

He considered his options. He had as much right to be here as they did, so he could simply walk out and take his chances that they'd leave him unmolested. He discarded that thought as patently absurd. He wasn't wanted here, and if the deputy was armed, what would stop him from shooting Bones and dropping his body into the pit or covering it in rocks and leaving it? No one would ever find him down here, of that he was certain.

That left stealth or main force as his avenues for escape.

The voices became clearer. He could tell for certain that two men were talking. He could make out a few stray words.

"...not in his hotel room..."

"...no way he found..."

"...somebody moved the rocks..."

They were talking about him. Time for action.

He picked up a short length of two-by-four from the pile of building materials, moved off to the side, and turned out his light.

Inky darkness enveloped him. The best night vision in the world was no good without at least a sliver of light. Fortunately, he was comfortable in the darkness and in confined spaces. He'd spent enough time in both over the years.

Soon, a faint glow announced the approach of someone carrying a light of some sort. Bones gripped the chunk of wood like a baseball bat and tensed.

"The pit's up here." The voice sounded like the deputy, though Bones couldn't be sure. "I don't see anyone."

"Maybe he's lost in one of the tunnels." A note of hopefulness rang in Matthew's voice.

"Probably. I'll take a look in here just to be sure." The deputy was looking back over his shoulder at Matthew when he stepped into the chamber and Bones took full advantage. He opted against the two-by-four and instead drove the heel of his palm into the man's temple with all his might. The deputy's knees buckled and Bones caught him and eased him to the ground. He hastily dragged the deputy off to the side, removed his boots, stuffed a sock into his mouth, and bound his wrists and ankles with his laces, and then extinguished the man's flashlight and laid it on the stack of lumber.

One down.

"Hector? You okay in there?" Matthew called a few moments later.

"Tripped and hit my head," Bones groaned, trying to add a touch of the deputy's accent to the words.

He heard hasty footsteps coming down the passageway. He resumed his position, and when Matthew strode into the chamber, Bones was ready. He cracked Matthew in the back of the head with the two-by-four. Matthew cried out and staggered forward a few steps. Bones struck again, baseball style, knocking Matthew's flashlight out of his hand and sending it spinning down into the pit.

The light vanished as the flashlight disappeared from sight.

"What the hell?" Matthew wailed.

Bones backed away from the sound of the man's voice, feeling for the passageway that would lead him out of the cavern. He'd love to stay and give Matthew the kind of beatdown a man who hits women so richly deserved, but decided against it. He'd assaulted a police officer, and a fight with Matthew, however brief, could leave marks on Bones that might identify him. Best to get while the getting was good.

He found the open passageway and moved quickly and silently until Matthew's curses faded away and he felt safe turning on his Maglite. He made the climb back to the surface as quickly as he could. It felt like an eternity, and when he finally emerged atop Halcón Rock, he fell to his knees, lungs heaving, clothing drenched with sweat. He spared only a few moments to rest before he pushed the slab of rock back over the hole that led into the pit.

He wondered how long it would take Matthew to feel around in the dark and find the deputy's flashlight. He hoped the idiot crawled off the edge of the pit by accident. He doubted he could be that lucky, but at least he'd made their lives difficult.

"Score one for the good guys."

EIGHT

A sharp rap at the door roused Bones from slumber. He rolled over and cracked one eye. The digital display on the cheap motel alarm clock read 8:08. Too early after the night he'd just had. He closed his eyes and pulled the covers over his head.

The knock came again.

"I don't need service today," he called.

"Sheriff's department."

A low groan of "holy crap" escaped his lips and he sat up. "Just a minute. I'm not dressed." He figured he didn't need to hurry. There was no back window or other means of escape, so it's not like the cops would be in a hurry to knock down the door and nab him before he slipped away. He pulled on jeans and a t-shirt and smoothed his hair back before opening the door.

He'd expected to see Hector, the deputy whom he'd knocked unconscious the night before, but the man who stood there was a solid fellow of late middle years. He was Anglo; his neatly-combed brown hair dusted with silver. His reflective sunglasses told Bones just how bad he looked after his late-night exertion and limited sleep.

"How can I help you?"

"I'm the sheriff." The man didn't provide his name, but his name tag read *W. Craig Jameson*. Bones didn't need a full night's sleep to put the pieces together. The man was Matthew's father. Great.

"Good to meet you." It was a lie, but Bones wasn't holding any cards in this situation, so he opted for courtesy.

Sheriff Jameson took off his glasses and tilted his head, inspecting Bones up and down with rheumy blue eyes. "You don't look so good. Have a late night?"

Bones forced a laugh. "If there's any nightlife here nobody told me about it. I'm just a late sleeper. I'm not at my best until lunchtime. Coffee helps, too."

Jameson nodded. "Can I come in? I need to ask you a few questions."

Bones stepped to the side and allowed the sheriff to come

inside. The man took a seat at the small window side table, and Bones took the chair opposite him.

"What's your business in Quemadura?"

"I don't have any. My truck broke down, and I'm waiting for Manny to get the parts in to fix it."

"Where are you headed?"

"Meeting friends in Vegas. I should have been there last night." He grimaced at the thought of Matt and Willis partying without him. He was missing it all: drinks, casinos, and the girls.

"I understand you were out at Halcón Rock yesterday." The sheriff arched an eyebrow.

"I went for a run and ended up at a rock formation. I guess that's the name of it."

"What were you doing out there?"

"Like I said, I went for a run, and that's where I ended up." Bones pushed back from the table. "You mind if I make some coffee while we talk? I can make you a cup, too." His thoughts were cloudy and he didn't want to slip up and say something that could implicate him in what happened last night.

"You go ahead. I'm fine." Jameson cleared his throat. "It seems a little strange that you would end up at Halcón Rock of all places. That's a restricted area."

"Not that strange," Bones said, keeping his back to the sheriff while he busied himself with the coffee maker. "It's public land and a nicer place to run than the highway. The rock was the only thing on the horizon, so I ran to it."

"That's a long way to run."

Bones shrugged. "I didn't have anything better to do."

"You had an incident with my deputy while you were there."

"If you call him telling me to leave and me complying an 'incident', then I guess so." Bones hit the button to start the coffee brewing and turned to face the sheriff. "I've got to ask. How can that be a restricted area if it's public land? No offense, but your deputy isn't a Fed and neither are you."

"Is that why you went back last night?" The question came sharp and fast, but Bones had been ready for it.

"I haven't been back. Dude told me to leave so I left."

Jameson folded his arms. "Why don't I believe you?"

"Probably because working in law enforcement doesn't exactly reinforce your faith in the human race." Bones smiled, but the sheriff didn't return it.

"Can anybody verify your whereabouts last night?"

"I don't know anybody except Manny." Behind him, the coffee maker began to sputter and spit, and the welcome aroma of brewing coffee filled the air.

"You know Mari."

"She gave me a ride when my car broke down. The only thing I really know about her is she's got a boyfriend who hits her."

Jameson flinched at that. Bones had drawn first blood. How would the sheriff respond?

"I'm going to be honest with you, Mister Bonebrake."

"That's always nice." Bones turned and busied himself with the coffee. He normally took it black, but he added cream and sugar just to kill a little time while Jameson stared at his back.

"I did some checking on you. For some reason, I could learn almost nothing about you. Why?"

"Maybe Google is not your friend?" Bones took a sip of coffee and locked eyes with the sheriff. He had to be careful here. If he followed his normal instincts, he might piss the guy off enough to get himself locked up on some bogus charge. Time to rein it in. "Actually, I'm ex-military, and I've been involved in a lot of sensitive stuff. I can't say for sure, but I think the powers-that-be have erased a lot of my history." That was half-true. A government agency had, in fact, gone to great lengths to hide much of his history, but that had mostly been done by Tam Broderick, head of the Myrmidon Squad, for reasons of her own.

Jameson nodded. "I did learn that you have an interest in aliens."

"Aliens, Nessie, Bigfoot, I love all that crap. Have since I was a kid."

"So you know the legends surrounding Halcón Rock." It wasn't a question. When Bones merely shook his head, the sheriff continued. "Some of your UFO-crazy friends have tried to say there were alien encounters there. It's based on an old Indian legend. Since you're both a UFO nut and an Indian, I have trouble believing you've never heard about it."

Bones took another sip of coffee to prevent himself from making a sarcastic reply. "First of all, I'm a Cherokee. Suggesting I'm related to the local native population would be like calling you Canadian just because you're white. Second, if I wanted to check out Halcón Rock, I'd do it. I wouldn't sabotage my transmission and cost myself a chunk of change when I'm supposed to be partying in Sin City with my friends."

Jameson stared, letting the conversation lapse. It was a common tactic. People had a natural urge to fill silences, and patient silence often proved more effective than asking questions. Bones knew that trick and many more. As a former Navy SEAL, he'd been trained to both to utilize and resist much more severe interrogation tactics than this. He stood there, drinking his coffee, until the sheriff relented.

Jameson stood and let out a long, slow breath.

"Mister Bonebrake, I know you went to Halcón Rock last night, and you assaulted two men. And when I can prove it, I'm going to make your life very unpleasant."

Bones merely smiled and waited for the man to see himself out. When the door closed behind Jameson, Bones let out a groan. Why did trouble always seem to find him?

NINE

Bones pulled into the parking lot of the University of New Mexico public library. Manny had taken pity on Bones and lent him the battered old pickup he called Consuela. She had no air conditioning and shimmied past sixty miles per hour, but Bones was delighted to be free of Quemadura, if only for a few hours.

Outside the library, he spared a moment to check out the scenery. Though it was an urban campus, the university had its share of green spaces that gave it that unique college flavor. The influences of southwestern architecture were all around. But he was mostly interested in the coeds. He smiled at a group of young women who were doing a poor job of hiding the fact that they were checking him out.

"How's your day going, ladies?" He flashed a disarming smile.

One young woman, a raven-haired Latina, bolder than the rest, broke off from her group. "Do you go to school here?"

"No, I'm just doing some research. You don't know anyone who could show me around the library, do you?"

She smiled. "I can help you. I just took my last exam for the semester." She looked up at him from beneath thick lashes. "I'm Yesenia, but everyone calls me Jessie."

"Everybody calls me Bones. You'll have to get to know me a lot better before I tell you my real name."

She laughed and led him into the library. Inside, they found a quiet table near a group of students who cast envious looks at Jessie. She turned and gave them a sarcastic wave, clearly loving the attention.

"So, what are we researching?" she whispered. "Definitely not physical fitness. I can tell you're already an expert at that." She immediately blushed and covered her face. "I'm sorry. My friends have been pushing me to come out of my shell. I'm a grad student, and I've had exactly two boyfriends since I've been here. Both of them possessive, controlling jerks."

"There seems to be a lot of that going around. Tell you what—one of them shows up, point him out to me and I'll put a scare into him."

"That won't be necessary. I can handle idiots just fine. It's the girly flirting stuff I'm lousy at."

"Cool. Well, there's no need to flirt with me. I'll be grateful for the help." Already he was revising his opinion of this attractive young woman, and feeling a touch guilty for having tried to charm his way into getting free library assistance. "I can even pay you for your time."

"Nah." Jessie dismissed the suggestion with a small wave. "If you don't turn out to be a creep I'll let you buy me coffee or lunch or something."

"Deal. Now, I need to research topics related to this." He took out his phone, called up the article on the incident on Halcón Rock, and handed it over to her.

Jessie stared at the screen for five seconds before pushing her chair back and fixing him with a speculative look. "Are you messing with me?"

"No. It's hard to explain. There are some people who believe this incident really happened." He omitted the fact that he was one of those people. "They're causing problems, and I want to understand why."

"So you think there's some kind of conspiracy?"

"Possibly. Local law enforcement is definitely keeping a close watch on the place. There must be a reason." He thought about the door he'd discovered beneath Halcón Rock and wished he could go back and investigate it further, but he figured the sheriff would keep that spot under close watch for a while.

"Okaaay." Jessie bit her lip and gazed down at the phone screen. "I doubt there will be any books on this subject, especially in the university library, but we'll see if we can't find something related to it." She logged on to a nearby computer, searched the catalog, and sent Bones off to retrieve a few select volumes on mysteries and legends of New Mexico while she searched online databases.

It took Bones a while to find the books he was looking for and by the time he returned Jessie had printed out a thick stack of articles.

"You owe me twenty bucks for printing charges."

"No sweat." He took out his money clip, peeled off two tens, and handed them over. "So, what did you find?"

"Truthfully, not a lot about the incident at Halcón Rock. I printed out all the articles I came across, but they're all superficial. Not as much as this one." She held up a copy of the original article Bones had shown her. "You should probably call this Amanda Shores lady. She seems to know the most about it."

"Yeah, I was hoping to avoid that. We dated for a while," he added, seeing her confused expression.

"It didn't end well?"

"It didn't really end. We just kind of stopped calling each other."

"That's crap. Somebody always ends it or causes it to end." Jessie folded her arms, emphasizing her cleavage, and Bones had to force himself not to stare. "Spill it. I'm not giving you any of this research until you tell me the story."

"Why do you care?" Bones couldn't help but chuckle.

"I'm interested. Now tell me."

"We live in different parts of the country, and I travel a lot, so we just kind of stopped calling each other."

Jessie narrowed her eyes. "You ghosted her, didn't you?"

"What does that mean?"

"It's when you disappear from someone's life like you're a ghost." She propped her chin on one hand and her gaze bored into him. "Did you stop calling? Leave it up to her to call or text you?"

"I guess so."

"Did you gradually take longer and longer to reply to her until one day you didn't reply at all?"

Bones sighed. "If this is what lunch conversation is going to be like, I think I'll just give you the cash and let you buy your own meal."

Jessie laughed. "Coward. Big, strong guy and you're afraid to call this girl after what you did to her."

"I'm not afraid. I just like to keep things chill, you know?"

The young woman rolled her eyes. "Whatever. Do you want the rest of this? They're articles on related topics: alien contact with Native Americans, people living under the earth, stuff like that."

"Cool, thanks."

They spent some time going over what she'd found. New

Mexico lore was filled with stories of alien visitors, and a surprising amount of material on underground dwellers, but none of it brought him any closer to learning what lay behind the door beneath Halcón Rock.

When they'd covered all the material, he checked his watch and declared it time to eat. He glanced toward the exit. "You know what kind of security they've got for these books? I think I'll snag a few of them."

"You're going to steal them?"

"I'll mail them a donation when I get home."

"No, you won't." Jessie shook her head, her long hair spilling over one shoulder. "For twenty-five dollars you can get a card that will let you check books out." She paused. "On second thought, I'll check them out for you. Then I'll get to see you one more time when you return the books. Unless you're going to treat me like you treated Amanda." She made a tiny pout.

"I don't think I could shake you if I wanted to. You seem tenacious for a girl your age."

"I'm twenty-four. I'm hardly a girl." She tossed her head and stood, her figure underscoring her point.

"My bad. So, how about we get out of here?"

"Text me your number first so I'll have it. I still don't completely trust you." She winked.

When they'd exchanged contact information, Jessie checked out the books Bones had retrieved. They headed back to the truck, Jessie regaling him with the virtues of Giovanni's Pizzeria, their lunch destination.

"It's to die for. It's been, like, in magazines and stuff. It's been voted the best in the state and makes top one hundred lists for best in the country. The neighborhood's kind of sketchy and there's always panhandlers hanging around the parking lot, so I never go there by myself, but I think you can handle it." She reached out and gave his bicep a squeeze. "Do you work out? Oh God, I did it again. I'm so awful at this."

Bones looked down at her, his expression serious. "You want my advice? Stop trying. You're smart, cute, and you seem like you've got attitude. You don't need to do anything for a guy. Make him come to you."

Jessie frowned. "Seriously?"

Bones nodded. "You haven't had many boyfriends because the average guy can't handle a girl who has it together. It's like the predator who picks off the young and weak. You're not an easy target, but that's okay."

"Are you calling me a wildebeest?"

Bones laughed and took her hand. "That's what I'm talking about. Attitude."

They arrived at the truck and Jessie froze. "Whose truck is this?"

"A dude named Manny. He lent it to me while he's working on mine."

"Consuela! I knew I recognized her." Jessie ran a hand lovingly across the hood of the old pickup. "Manny's my great uncle. So that means you broke down in Quemadura. Not much to do there."

"Except piss off the sheriff."

"Craig? If you're on his bad side, that speaks well of you. Have you met his son?"

Bones nodded.

If Jessie had anything to say about Matthew, she didn't get the chance. Two men, one blond, one red-haired, dressed in white button-up shirts, ties, and black pants, approached them. Bones first thought was the two were Mormon missionaries, but he dismissed the thought. They were too old to fit the profile, each in their early thirties. Furthermore, they carried themselves with a bearing recognizable only to those who had spent a significant amount of time in the military. Both appeared to be sizing up Bones as they approached. Something was weird here.

"Good afternoon," the redhead began, "we're special investigators with the New Mexico State Police Department. You conducted Internet searches that triggered security warnings. We need you to turn over any material you gathered, and the two of you will have to come with us."

"No problem. Here you go." Bones flung the stack of books at the two men, sprang forward, and drove his fist into the redhead's jaw. The man's legs turned to rubber and, as he fell, Bones delivered a spinning back fist to the temple of the blond man, who had stood temporarily frozen in surprise at the suddenness and fury of his attack. "Jessie, get in the truck!" he shouted.

She dashed to the other side of the vehicle and tried the handle. "It's locked!"

Bones fished the keys out of his pocket. From the direction of the library he saw a uniformed man trotting in their direction. Campus security was on its way, which meant the police wouldn't be far behind. No time to search the fallen men. In fact, the redhead was already sitting up. "Crap." He scooped up the library books, knowing they could be traced back to Jessie, and tossed them into the truck bed. He hastily unlocked the truck, jumped inside, and let Jessie in.

"Why did you attack those guys?" she demanded over the roar of the engine as he fired up Consuela and threw her into reverse.

"I don't know who those guys are, but they aren't law enforcement." Tires squealed, and Consuela fishtailed as he floored the gas pedal.

"How can you be sure?" Jessie asked.

Bones glanced in the rear-view mirror. The two men had regained their feet. As he watched, the blond reached into his waistband and drew a handgun.

"The fact that they're trying to kill us is a pretty good clue. Get down!"

TEN

Bones hit the accelerator and yanked the pickup hard to the left as shots rang out. Jessie screamed and covered her head. Bones forced her down to the floorboard and then yanked the truck back to the right. The rear window shattered and Jessie screamed again.

"Un-be-freaking-lievable!" he shouted. He downshifted and took the truck up over the curb and onto the grassy expanse of a small public park. He took out a garbage can, sending its contents flying through the air. Pedestrians scattered, shouting curses, as the truck lurched and skidded past. Bones weaved in and of the few trees, wishing for more cover, but no more shots came.

When they crossed the park and bounced down onto a busy street to the blaring of horns, Jessie dared to peek her head back up.

"Did we get away?"

"I don't know. Maybe. Do you see anyone coming?"

Jessie looked behind them. "Lots of people are behind us, but no one seems to be… uh oh."

"What?" A cold fist squeezed Bones' gut as he turned to follow her line of sight. A sleek, black Jaguar was shooting across the park. "Just great," he muttered.

"We're never going to get away from them in this traffic," Jessie said. "Get over to the right and you can get on the highway."

"We don't want the highway," Bones said as he whipped over to the right to pass the slow-moving delivery truck in front of him.

"Why not?"

"Consuela will never outrun that Jag. Out on the highway, they'll catch up with us in seconds. At least in town, the traffic will slow them down too."

"Unless they drive down the wrong side of the road."

"What?" A quick glance in the side-view mirror elicited a stream of profanity. The Jaguar was zipping along on the wrong side of the road, quickly closing the distance between them.

"What do we do?" Jessie cried.

Bones didn't answer. He whipped Consuela back over into the right lane. To his left, the nose of the Jaguar appeared just ahead of the front bumper of the truck Bones had just passed. The passenger window appeared, and then a fist holding an automatic pistol. Bones stamped on the brake pedal as the passenger opened fire. Behind him, tires squealed and horns blared. He hit the gas and tried to keep the truck between him and the Jaguar.

On the opposite side of the road, cars were whipping to the side to get out of the way of the fast-moving vehicle. The Jaguar dropped back behind the truck, and the passenger fired again. The shots went wide, whumping into the side of the delivery truck. At this, the truck driver panicked and skidded to a halt.

A series of squeals and crashes filled the air as the vehicles behind the truck careened into one another. Bones hoped everyone was all right, but he couldn't worry about that right now. He and Jessie had lost the scant protection the truck had provided and were now exposed.

"Here goes nothing." He accelerated and veered to the left, bounding over the median and heading right for the Jaguar.

It shouldn't have worked. The gunman in the passenger seat should have taken careful aim and ended Bones, but like most people, he lacked the complete focus required to use a weapon effectively in such a situation. Hitting a moving target was difficult enough, shooting accurately while moving was even tougher, but doing it while your target was trying to kill you was something altogether different. His shot went wide and then the driver panicked and hit the brakes.

Bones didn't have time to celebrate as the Jaguar skidded and fishtailed. A major intersection loomed up ahead, and he was on the wrong side of the road. There was no time to correct his course. Instead, he pounded the gas and held down the horn.

"Everybody out of the freaking way!" he shouted, not that anyone could hear him. He zipped through the red light, barely missed being sideswiped by an ugly, yellow VW Beetle, and then shot directly into the path of an oncoming big rig. They missed one another by inches, the rig's horn blaring its deep cry. Bones took a hard left below a street sign that read LOMAS.

"Do you know where Lomas takes us?" he called to Jessie, who had returned to the passenger seat but held her hands over her face.

"Which way? East or west?"

"I don't know, let me think. The big mountain is behind us, so we're going west."

She shrugged. "No idea."

"What if we went east?"

"No clue."

Bones frowned. "Then why did you ask which way we were going?"

"I don't know. I've never been shot at before, jerk!" She uncovered her face, balled a fist, and punched him in the shoulder. "If you keep going you'll hit the Rio Grande."

"I doubt we can swim for it," Bones said, managing a smile. In this part of the country, the Rio Grande was shallow enough to wade across.

"I don't suppose there's any chance they'll give up?" Jessie turned to look out the shattered back window. "Never mind. They're way back there, but they're coming."

"Holy crap," Bones grumbled.

"They're on the right side of the road this time. I guess that's a good thing?"

"I was kind of hoping they'd have a head-on collision with a cement truck, but that was overly optimistic."

"Should we get off the main road? We might lose them."

"Or we might end up sitting ducks on a dead-end street." He gritted his teeth and concentrated on working his way through traffic. He caught a glimpse of the Jaguar in his rearview mirror. Like Jessie had said, it was coming after them. He knew he couldn't outrun them. Something had to give.

Up ahead, a U-Haul truck was camped out in the left lane, feeding a steady stream of traffic into the right lane as vehicles moved to pass it. It was causing a major slowdown—not what he needed. Then again, it might afford an opportunity. He set his jaw and, riding inches from the bumper of the car in front of him, made his slow way past the moving truck, and then whipped over right in front of it. The driver of the U-Haul blew his horn, but Bones ignored him. He checked his mirrors and confirmed that the Jaguar was out of sight.

"Just give me a curve or something," he muttered.

Seconds later, the road curved to the right, cutting them off from the view of all but the vehicles closest behind them. Bones seized the opportunity. He cut left across oncoming traffic and onto a two-lane road and floored it. The engine roared as Consuela chugged down the street. Not daring to hope he'd lost their pursuers, he made another left, glancing back as he turned.

"Damn!"

"They're still after us?" Jessie asked.

Bones nodded. "Either they saw us turn, or they made a lucky guess. Either way, this isn't over."

They sped along the street, the old truck moving much too slowly for Bones' liking. While he concentrated on the road, Jessie kept an eye out for the Jaguar. All too soon, she delivered the bad news.

"They're really close. You need to do something."

"Not many choices," he said through gritted teeth. "You got your seatbelt on?"

"Yeah, why?"

He didn't answer. Instead, he yanked the wheel and shot recklessly through oncoming traffic. He was now almost deaf to the sounds of squealing tires and blaring horns, but he was keenly aware of the van that skidded to a halt inches from the passenger door.

"Are you trying to kill me?" Jessie shrieked.

"The opposite." He said as they shot past a statue of a horse and rider, and a sign that read *Old Town Albuquerque*. "Just trying to get some distance between us before they start…"

He cut off in mid-sentence when a bullet shattered the driver's side mirror.

"Shooting," he added. He kept the pedal to the floor, trying to coax more speed out of the aging pickup, but moments later he slammed on the brakes. "Oh, hell no."

The street up ahead was clogged with pedestrians. He hit the horn, threw the truck into low gear, and surged forward. Surprised tourists gave way, sending dirty looks, obscene gestures, and curses in his direction.

"This is not where we want to be," Jessie said.

Up ahead, the road wound around a small square. A mariachi band played in the gazebo at the center of the square, and tourists lounged all about, enjoying the music. A myriad of shops and restaurants lined the square, and vendors dotted the sidewalks, selling food or Native American trinkets. To their left, an old mission church dominated the square; tourists queued up in front waiting their turn to go inside. Many turned to gape at the old truck as it skidded recklessly around the square.

When they reached the opposite side of the square, Bones hung a sharp right, blowing through the stop sign, and coming face-to-face with a VW bus.

"Wrong way!" Jessie cried.

"I know that now!" Bones shouted as he brought the truck up onto the sidewalk, narrowly missing the vehicle. A man in a sombrero and serape dove out of their way, upending his taco cart as he fell. Bones managed to miss the cart, but brought the truck back into oncoming traffic.

"What are you doing?"

"I'm not wasting good Mexican food!" Bones zigzagged out of the way of two angry drivers and took the first available turn. He kept going, making turns at random, but the Jaguar stayed in their rear-view mirror.

"We're not going to lose them, are we?"

"Don't say that. We can…"

The truck began to lose speed. Bones pumped the pedal, but nothing happened. He looked down and immediately spotted the problem.

"Why are we stopping?" Jessie asked, looking around for the Jag.

"Um." He couldn't look her in the eye as he spoke. "We're out of gas."

ELEVEN

Bones yanked the wheel, steered the truck over to the side of the road, and brought it to a skidding halt on a patch of hard-packed dirt beneath the shade of an old oak tree. To their left, a high chain link fence topped with razor wire ran as far as the eye could see in both directions. To their right, on the other side of the street, lay a mobile home park.

Jessie moved to cross the street, but Bones grabbed her by the arm. "No. That's where they'll expect us to go, and there's no cover."

"Where else is there?"

"Follow me." He clambered up into the bed of the pickup truck, then up onto the top of the cab. Directly above them hung a fat tree limb, which extended beyond the fence. "Can you make it?" he asked.

"I was a gymnast in high school. I think I can handle it."

"That's what I'm talking about." He cupped his hands and gave her a boost.

Jessie swung up onto the limb with a strength and grace Bones could not help but admire. She quickly scrambled along the length of the limb, well past the coils of razor wire, until the limb began to sag beneath her weight.

"Aren't you coming?" she called back.

"As soon as you're down. I'm afraid it won't hold both of us."

Jessie didn't argue. She swung down, dangled in midair for a moment, and then dropped to the ground. As soon as she let go, Bones followed. He had just crossed the fence when Jessie called out a warning.

"Here they come!"

He didn't' need to look back. The screech of tires and hum of the engine told him all he needed to know. There was no time to climb a safe distance. He dropped down as soon as he cleared the fence line. The impact sent sharp pain lancing up his legs and along his spine. He forced himself to his feet, knees screaming in protest, and took Jessie's hand.

"Where to?"

"Down the hill. There are some trees and bushes that will give us some cover." He took her hand and led the way.

They scrambled and skidded their way down the steep embankment. Up above, their pursuers screeched to a stop. Car doors slammed, and voices rang out.

"Which way did they go?"

"Try that way."

Bones hoped "that way" meant the trailer park. That would hopefully buy them some time.

At the bottom of the slope, they hit a thick stand of brush and trees. Bones forced his way through and let out a cry of surprise when he stepped out into open space.

"Crap!" He snagged the nearest bush, a scraggly juniper, and steadied himself. He stood at the edge of a concrete moat a good fifteen feet across and twenty feet deep. "What the hell?"

He didn't have time to inspect his surroundings any farther because Jessie banged into his back, knocking him forward.

"Hold on, chick!" he said, steadying himself again as he teetered on the edge of the precipice.

"Uh oh." Jessie's head peeked out under his outstretched arm. "End of the line. What is this place?"

"Some kind of drainage ditch, I guess. It doesn't matter what it is. We have to find a way across." Bones' eyes searched the gray, concrete channel. On the other side lay another stand of greenery. More cover if they could only find a way over.

The voices from the street rose again, closer this time.

"Do you think they went over the fence?"

"Damn!" Bones took Jessie's hand and inched along the edge of the channel. A few agonizing feet along, he stumbled.

"Hey, don't take me down with you," Jessie said.

"I tripped." He looked down and smiled. An old, aluminum extension ladder peeked out from the thick undergrowth. "But I think we've found our way across." He took hold of the ladder and heaved, and it tore free with a sound of ripping vegetation that was too loud for his liking.

"We're going to climb down and back up again?" A note of doubt hung in Jessie's voice.

"Too slow. We're going to make a bridge out of this baby." Carefully, he stretched the ladder out to its full length.

He could see now that it was a sixteen-footer. It might make it across. Might.

Carefully, he extended the ladder across the precipice. It clanged down on the concrete lip at the far side of the moat with six inches or so to spare on either side. He heard the rattle of the chain link fence at the top of the hill. The idiots who were chasing them hadn't figured out to use the tree to get across. At least, not yet.

"Okay," he said to Jessie, "go for it. You're a gymnast so just pretend it's a balance beam, and you'll be okay."

"Why am I going first?" She eyed the ladder with suspicion.

"I weigh over two hundred pounds. If that thing breaks while I'm on it, I'm down in the pit with a broken leg, and you're stuck on the same side of the pit as those assclowns." He inclined his head in the direction from which they had come.

"Makes sense, but if this thing doesn't hold me, I swear I will haunt you 'til your dying day."

"If the ladder doesn't hold, my dying day will be here in a few minutes. Go!"

Jessie squeezed past him and stepped a tentative foot out onto the ladder. It gave an inch and then held. She let out a breath he hadn't known she'd been holding, extended her arms to either side and stepped out with her other foot.

"Don't look down," he cautioned.

"Shut up. You're distracting me." He grinned despite the dire circumstances and watched with admiration as she made her way across.

"Hey, we can climb up on the truck and climb over on that tree limb," a voice shouted. Oh well. They had to figure it out soon or later.

As soon as Jessie stepped off the ladder, Bones mounted it. It creaked under his weight, but he didn't hesitate. He made it across, or he died. He took another step and then another. The ladder sagged, and he felt it collapsing beneath him. He took a big step and then leaped forward. His makeshift bridge gave all at once and dropped with a noisy clang to the floor of the moat.

"Somebody's down there!" one of the men at the top of the hill called. A bullet pinged the wall of the ditch and ricocheted wildly as the report of a pistol reached their ears.

"I really wish I had my Glock," Bones muttered. "Come on."

He turned and forced his bulk into the dense stand of foliage and they found themselves at the top of a ten-foot wall. Down below lay an open, grassy area interspersed with a few dirt patches and boulders.

"A park," Jessie said, peeking around his shoulder. "We need to get across before they catch up with us."

"I don't think this is...whoa!" He was cut short when Jessie gave him a hard, unexpected shove in the small of the back and he found himself flying through the air. For the second time, he hit the ground hard, every joint screaming in pain. He was going to break something if he kept this up.

He turned to see Jessie dangling from the lip of the wall. He tried to call out a warning, but she dropped to the ground before he could form the words. She grinned down at him.

"Get off your butt and let's move before those guys find a way across the..." Her words died on her lips as the blood drained from her face.

"That's what I was trying to tell you," Bones said. Out of the corner of his eye, he saw two large, tawny shapes padding toward them.

"This isn't a park. It's a zoo."

TWELVE

Bones spread his arms and backed slowly toward Jessie, his eyes flitting between the lion and lioness that were moving toward them. He'd had some experience with wild animals, even predators, but he had a feeling what worked on a bear wouldn't work on these apex predators from the savanna.

"Oh my God," Jessie whimpered. "What are we going to do?"

"No sudden moves," he said. "And try not to show any fear."

"It's all I can do not to faint. How am I supposed to show no fear?"

"Just do your best. Remember, zoo employees work with these animals all the time, so it's not like we're encountering them in the wild." That was technically true, but Bones knew it to be a flimsy hope. Nothing would change the fact that these were wild animals at heart.

"They are beautiful," Jessie managed. "If I wasn't about to die from fear and shock, I might want to give one a hug."

"Same here," Bones lied. Right now, he wanted nothing more than to get away. He stole a glance over his shoulder and saw that they were about twenty meters from an access door. It would be locked, but hopefully, someone would see them here, and an employee would let them out. "Follow me." Keeping his eyes on the big cats and Jessie between himself and the wall, he began inching to his left, toward the door.

"I wonder what the tourists are thinking," Jessie said.

Bones glanced toward the front of the exhibit and realized they were screened from view by a huge boulder and the corner of a wall. No one knew they were here. "I don't know."

The big male paused, sniffed the air, and gave a great shake of his mane. The female crept a few paces closer before also pausing and giving an audible sniff.

"What are they doing?"

"I don't know," Bones said. "Just keep moving."

The door seemed to be no closer as they made their slow way through the lion habitat, but the lions made no move to follow them, and a flicker of hope sparked inside him. Maybe they could make it.

Just then, the male let out a low rumble, every muscle in its body tensed.

Holy crap, he thought. So close.

"If either of them makes a move for us, I want you to run for the door," he said.

"But what about you?"

There was no time to answer. Voices rang out from the direction of the road. Someone shouted, "There they are!"

Bones looked up to see the two men who'd been pursuing them standing on the wall at the back of the habitat. The red haired man raised his pistol and took aim.

"Run!" Bones gave Jessie a shove and then sprang to the side as the man squeezed the trigger. The bullet pinged off the wall behind him, a foot from his head. The lions broke and ran at the sound of the shot, heading for safety behind the boulder that dominated the small space. Bones zigged and zagged as he ran for the door, suddenly wishing he were a runt like his friend Maddock, and not a six foot five behemoth. Another shot rang out and then another. Both missed.

Jessie was tugging at the doorknob, but they were locked in.

"Move!" Bones thundered. He leaped, twisted in the air, and drove both feet into the door in a devastating flying side kick. The door didn't budge, and he found himself lying on the ground, pain coursing through his legs.

The door flew open, and a young man in the khaki garb of a zoo employee poked his head out.

"What is going on out here?" He cried out in shock as a bullet punched through the door inches from his nose. Bones shouldered him aside and hauled Jessie through the doorway. They dashed away, his cries chasing them down the dimly-lit concrete passageway.

They ran blindly through the building, winding through the corridors until at last they found an EXIT door and emerged in the middle of a surprised-looking group of zoo workers.

"What are you two doing in there?" a sturdy woman of middle years demanded.

"Got lost," Bones said. He took Jessie by the elbow and steered her around the confused group.

"Hold on a minute. How did you even…" The woman moved to block their path, but Bones froze her with what he liked to call his "Lethal Weapon eyes," modeled after the crazed expressions of Mel Gibson's character. The man was a douche in real life, but he pulled off the borderline lunatic role with ease. As the lady gave way, she mumbled to her companions, "Call security."

Bones and Jessie quickened their pace and wove through the crowd until they were out of sight of the employees. None had dared follow them.

"Head for the front gate?" Jessie asked.

Bones shook his head. "That's where security is likely to wait for us. And I'll bet one of our friends with the guns back there is waiting for us there while the other watches the truck. We need another way out."

"Such as?"

He scanned the area and quickly spotted what he was looking for. "Over there, behind the concession stand." He pointed to a delivery truck idling behind the concession area, just in front of a locked gate that opened onto an access road. The snow-capped peak of the Rocky Mountains was painted on the sign with the word "Coors" emblazoned across them in red. It wasn't Dos Equis, but it would do.

"A beer truck?" Jessie asked. "Is this really the time?"

"Just follow my lead." They hurried over to the concession stand and stopped a few paces from the truck. Bones watched as the deliveryman unloaded a few cases, stowed his hand truck, and then headed inside the concession stand, clipboard in hand.

"Come on," Bones said. They hurried over to the truck, double-checked to make sure the coast was clear, and then clambered into the back of the vehicle. The cold air of the refrigerated truck gave him the chills, but he didn't care. He just wanted to get away safely and then figure out their next move. He hastily rearranged some crates, and he and Jessie hunkered down behind them.

"It's freezing in here." She scooted over and pressed her body against his. He put an arm around her and pulled her close, trying not to let his thoughts drift to her trim, athletic figure and her soft hair.

"You're not going to make a move on me, are you?"

"What? Oh, no. At least, not until we get away."

"Fair enough. We'll put a pin in that discussion and circle back to it later."

Bones grinned. He liked this girl.

Behind them, the truck door clanged shut, and their surroundings went black. Moments later, the engine roared to life, and the truck lurched forward.

"So, how do we get Manny's truck back?" Jessie asked.

"I'm not sure. Maybe give it a day and then call a tow truck. They won't stand guard there forever." He paused and scratched his chin. "One thing I can't figure. They clearly wanted our research, so why did they come after us once we abandoned the truck? You'd think they'd look inside."

"They won't find the research there. I stuffed it all inside my shirt when we took off. Feel the small of my back."

Bones slid his hand around and, sure enough, felt the thick sheaf of papers there.

"Way to think on your feet. I'm impressed."

Just then the truck took a sharp turn, throwing Jessie hard against Bones.

"Not the smoothest ride," she said.

"No, but we're safe."

"How can you be so calm? We've been chased, shot at, almost eaten by lions, and you're so…chill, and I don't mean because it's cold in here."

Bones laughed. "Chick, you wouldn't believe the things I've been through."

THIRTEEN

As luck would have it, the driver's next stop was Giovanni's Pizzeria, Jessie's restaurant of choice. She and Bones slipped out unseen and worked their way around to the front lot. Located in a rundown strip mall, the savory aromas wafting from the restaurant were, in Bones' opinion, the only things to recommend the location. He scanned the area, just to make sure their pursuers hadn't somehow figured out their means of escape and followed them, but all he saw were a few people begging for change, and an obvious drug deal going down in the corner of the parking lot.

Inside, they settled into a booth adorned with a red and white checked tablecloth and ordered up two Dos Equis and a pepperoni and green chile pizza. While they waited for their food, Bones kept an eye on the parking lot while Jessie quietly gave him an overview of her research.

"The hollow earth legend has been around for a long time," she began. "Basically, there are two competing theories: one is that humans or a species very much like humans live beneath the earth. The other is that aliens live, or once lived, there; maybe observing us, maybe interbreeding with humans to form the modern human race." She rolled her eyes.

Bones wondered how she would react if he told her about some of the thing he had seen and experience in that regard.

"Come on." She reached across the table and poked his arm. "No mocking comments?"

"For the sake of argument, let's say we're considering all possibilities."

"All right." Jessie smirked and returned to her papers. "The Nazis were particularly invested in this theory. They considered several places as likely locations for the entrance to the world beneath, including Tibet, the North Pole, and Antarctica." She frowned. "This is interesting. They sent large expeditions to Antarctica, tons of scientists, and none of them were ever heard from again."

"I'm not trying to rush you or anything," Bones said, "but I've heard this before, and it doesn't really help me with Halcón

Rock."

"In that case, I won't bother covering any of this." Jessie thumbed through her papers and slid about half of them to the side.

"Sorry, I promise I'll read them later. What else have you got?"

"Have you heard of the Ant People?"

Bones shook his head. "Just the dude from the movie."

"Good. Then don't interrupt this time." She gave him a sly wink. "Hopi legend tells of two cataclysms: fire and ice."

"Maybe a comet and an ice age?"

"I told you not to interrupt. Both times, the virtuous members of the Hopi were guided to safety, following a cloud by day and a burning star by night. Sound familiar?"

"You said not to interrupt."

"It's not interrupting if I ask you a question."

"Sure, the Exodus story."

"Very good." Jessie grinned mischievously. "The cloud and the star guided them to the Ant People, or Anu Sinom in their language. The Ant People took them into their subterranean caves and nurtured and fed them. It's believed that the kiva, the Puebloans' underground center of worship, was inspired by the distant memory of the safety their people found beneath the earth."

Bones nodded and scratched his chin. Jessie had fallen silent, so he felt safe speaking. "Interesting that they don't claim there's a hollow earth down there, just caves and caverns. That's much more believable."

Jessie nodded. "The ant people are memorialized in pictographs. I printed out a couple." She pushed two sheets over to Bones.

The images were of slender beings with long heads and bulbous eyes. "The shape of the head reminds me of the Paracelsus Skulls," he mused.

"And what about this one?" She tapped the last image. "Look at what he's wearing." Unlike the other images, this figure seemed to be wearing a rectangular box covered in lines, dots, and circles. "It looks like a space suit, doesn't it?"

"I think you're reaching, but point taken. What else do you have?"

"The legend extends, in different forms, to other native peoples of the Southwest. The legends vary in the details, but all associate the underworld dwellers with the constellation Orion."

That got Bones' attention. Several times in recent years he and his partner, Dane Maddock, had come across compelling evidence that connected Orion with alien visitors to Earth.

"Something wrong? You flinched?"

"No, I'm fine. Go on."

"There's not much else here. Unless you care that the Hopi religious leaders refer to the Ant People as "Ant Friends" or "anu-naki.""

Bones dropped his beer bottle. It hit the table with a sharp crack and he barely caught it before it tipped over."

"What is your deal?" Jessie leaned back a little, eyes boring into him from beneath a furrowed brow. "Post-traumatic stress?"

He chuckled and shook his head. "The Sumerians had a word for the beings that once came to Earth from outer space. They called them the Annunaki."

"Really? That's pretty cool. Anyway, there's a little more here about possible links to Egypt. The word for star is the same in both languages. Stuff like that." She shuffled her papers. "To summarize, this part of the country has a strong oral tradition regarding contact with aliens or alien-like creatures. Some are UFO stories, but many are tales of contact with beings living underground."

Their food arrived, and they dug in. Bones had to admit it was some of the best pizza he'd ever tasted. The chiles were fresh and perfectly cooked, the crust just the right balance between soft and crispy.

While they ate, Bones considered what Jessie had told him. The legends alone would be scant evidence of alien contact, but having seen the door beneath Halcón rock, he had little trouble believing it.

"I don't get it," Jessie finally said. "This Halcón Rock thing is clearly just another legend. You seem like a smart guy, but you're taking this stuff pretty seriously. Why?"

Bones took a drink to buy himself some time. He'd been in this sort of situation before, and his options weren't great.

He could let her think him a fool who believed in fairy tales, or he could tell her the truth about some of the mind-blowing archaeological finds he and Maddock had made, none of which he could prove for various reasons, and be thought a liar or crazy.

"Do you trust me?" he asked.

Jessie bit her lip and gazed at him through half-closed eyes. Finally, she began to slowly nod. "I do."

"All right. Will you take me at my word that alien contact, even aliens living underground, is not just possible, but probable?"

"Nope. You'll have to show me proof."

Bones shook his head. "Can't blame you for that, but I can't do it."

"Why not? You're not just giving up the chase, are you?"

"Not at all, but I'm going to get you back to school and Manny's truck back to him before I do anything else."

"Excuse me? I can't go back to school." She held up a hand before he could interrupt. "Can you honestly say I'm safe from whoever came after us? Do you even know who they are or what they want?"

"No, but I have an idea who sent them." In his mind, it was a no-brainer that either Matthew or the sheriff was behind this. Anything else would be far too great a coincidence.

"Good for you. Can you promise me they won't try to get information out of me, or use me to get to you?"

Bones stared into Jessie's eyes, trying to think of a single point of disagreement, but she was right. He let his shoulders fall, and he slumped back in his seat.

"You know, for a college kid you're really something?"

Jessie's eyes were immediately afire. "I'm not a kid. I'm twenty-four years old."

"Okay, sorry." He raised his hands to ward off her flinty gaze. "I'm just getting old, so everybody under thirty looks young to me." It was lame, but all he could think of at the moment. The girl was pretty, smart, and a lot more tenacious than he'd expected.

"You're not that much older than me," she reproved. "Now, I'll call AAA and have them tow Manny's truck to a dealership I know, then we'll go get my car and head up to

Santa Fe."

Bones cocked his head. "That's the wrong direction, chick."

"Not for what I've got planned." Jessie flashed a wicked grin. "We're going to talk to Amanda Shores."

FOURTEEN

The offices of the Santa Fe Sun overlooked the plaza in the center of the old part of town. Tourists milled about, exploring the art galleries and examining the wares of the Native American vendors set up along the sidewalks. Nestled in the foothills of the Sangre De Cristo mountains, Santa Fe, at least the older sections, carried upon it the weight of history and a strong sense of Southwestern culture.

Bones paused at the door and turned around.

"What are you doing?" Jessie asked as she tried to follow his line of sight.

"Just taking in the scenery. Nice place." He closed his eyes and breathed in the strong aroma of meat, beans, and chile wafting from a food cart nearby. "We should get a Navajo taco. Those things are awesome."

Jessie laughed and took his hand in both of hers. "Quit stalling. We're supposed to meet Amanda in five minutes." She raised an eyebrow. "Are you really that nervous about seeing an ex-girlfriend?"

"Not really," he lied. "Like I told you before, I keep things chill, and Amanda isn't known to be a chill person. At least, not when you get on the wrong side of her."

"Based on our time spent together, I'm having trouble putting you and chill together."

"You caught me on a weird day." He opened the door for her and followed her inside. A young Latino man greeted them at the front desk and buzzed Amanda, who appeared all too quickly. She'd probably been waiting in the hall, ready to swoop.

Amanda hadn't changed a bit. She was still the raven-haired, statuesque beauty he remembered. She stood, hands on hips, gazing imperiously at Bones. Though she was several inches shorter than he, it felt as if she were looking down at him.

"Bones." She somehow managed to speak his name as if it simultaneously amused and disgusted her. "It only took you how many years to return my last call?"

Bones flashed his most roguish grin. "You know how it is. Maddock and I…"

"I know exactly how it is. You're a jerk." She shot a glance at Jessie, her eyes taking the young woman in, assessing her. "I was going to let you have it the moment I laid eyes on you, but I'll cut you some slack in front of your girlfriend. I suppose one of us ought to have a little class."

"We're just friends," Jessie said to Amanda's back as the reporter stalked away down the hall, motioning for them to follow.

Her office was small and neatly appointed. A laptop and desk calendar sat atop a polished wooden desk. Behind her hung a shelf lined with *Dia de los Muertos*-themed figurines. The skeletal figures, garbed in the traditional attire of the Spanish colonial era, danced, played instruments, or went about ordinary tasks. Bones found it a macabre yet somehow engaging scene.

"That would make one hell of a Christmas village," he noted.

"I have a Santa, but I don't bring him out until the day after Thanksgiving."

Bones nodded, not sure how to begin. A framed photo in the windowsill, a shot of Amanda standing atop a red rock formation, caught his eye. "Hey! You cropped me out of that picture."

Amanda smirked. "It's a good shot of me."

Bones nodded. "Every picture of you is…"

"Don't!" Amanda held up a hand. "I don't want any of your banter or flirtatious crap. I also don't want to hear about how Maddock dumped Jade for your sister."

Jade Ihara was an archaeologist and a former girlfriend of Bones' partner and best friend, Dane Maddock. A few years earlier, the four of them had been caught up together in one of Maddock and Bones' adventures.

"How did you know about that?"

"Jade calls me every now and then."

Bones scratched his chin. "I thought you two didn't like each other all that much."

"We discovered we have something in common. We're both attracted to jerks."

"So you *are* still attracted to me." Bones flashed another grin which did nothing to crack Amanda's icy exterior.

Beside him, Jessie let out an exasperated sigh. "Is he always like this?"

Amanda regarded her coolly. "You mean you haven't figured it out yet?"

"We only met yesterday. I'm sticking with him because I think I might get killed if I don't. Somebody's after him… after *us*."

"That sounds all too familiar." Amanda rounded on Bones. "Can't you, for once, solve one of your little mysteries without getting innocent girls caught up with you?"

"Hey, you love a mystery as much as I do, and you know it."

Amanda held up her hands. "Whatever. This is a waste of our time. You wanted to know about the incident at Halcón Rock?"

"Or anything related to it. Here's what we have." Jessie gave Amanda a quick overview of their research and the conclusions they had drawn thus far.

"I can't add much," Amanda said. "A few stories told to me in confidence by Los Alamos employees. All seem to agree that some sort of human-like creatures live underground, but there's no evidence. No one could show me a single photograph or artifact. Nothing. Before I met Bones, I would have thought it was all a bunch of crap, and I'm still leaning in that direction, but I can't dismiss it entirely."

"Why are you gathering information if you don't buy into it?" Jessie asked.

"It's because of the article I wrote. I thought of it as a fluff piece, but ever since the newspaper ran the story, I've gotten a steady stream of conspiracy buffs and self-described informants knocking at my door. She turned her gaze onto Bones, who shifted in his seat.

"So, if you don't have anything for us, why did I make the drive up here?" Bones asked. "Just to give me a hard time?"

"I know you, Bones, and you haven't put all your cards on the table yet."

"Look, we had a good time together, but the long distance thing isn't for me."

"You know what I mean. A single Native American legend isn't enough to set you on a search, and it certainly isn't enough for you to yet again run afoul of dangerous people. Now, are you going to sit here blowing smoke signals up my ass or are you going to tell me the whole truth?"

"That's racist," Bones muttered. That didn't get a rise out of her. "Fine. I found a hidden passageway beneath Halcón Rock." He went on to describe the door he had found and the chamber in which it was located. "I'd like to get back there, and maybe I could, but right now the sheriff is watching the place, and I suspect he's the reason these other guys are after me."

Amanda stared at him for the span of three heartbeats. Finally, she nodded. "Okay, I believe you. And if there really is an alien doorway…"

"I'd call it a high-tech doorway," Bones said. "We can't say for certain it's alien in origin."

"If you say so. Anyway, I've got a few leads I've actually considered following up on, but I didn't want to waste my time. If you've seen this doorway, that's good enough for me. There might be a story in it, maybe even a book."

"Cool. Just give me the leads and I'll follow up on them for you."

Amanda laughed. "Not a chance. Like it or not, you and I are working together again."

FIFTEEN

"What the hell is going on with Manny's truck?" Matthew glanced at his father, who gazed impassively at the tow truck pulling the battered pickup into the parking lot of Manny's service center. The back window was shattered, but otherwise, it seemed to be no more beaten up that it had been when Bonebrake had driven it out of town the previous day.

"Bonebrake had to ditch it," Sheriff Jameson said. "I guess he had it towed back here."

Matthew rounded on him, hands on hips. "How do you know he ditched it?"

"Settle yourself, son. We'll talk about this in private." Jameson turned and strode toward his patrol car.

Matthew glowered at his father's back. The man still treated him like a kid, not just demanding but assuming complete obedience. Did he follow along meekly, or did he stand here like a contrary child? He couldn't win. Fists clenched, he stalked over to the car and climbed in.

"I had a couple of my friends check on Bonebrake," the sheriff said as he pulled the car out onto the road.

"Why did you do that?" Matthew pounded his fist on the dashboard. "This is my project! Mine!"

The sheriff slowly turned his head toward Matthew. That was all it took to subdue him. Though his father wore mirrored sunglasses, Matthew could feel the man's steely eyes boring into him. No one else in his life had this effect on him, and he hated it.

"I didn't tell them anything about your project. I just gave them the scent and they…overdid it on the pursuit."

Matthew's shoulders sagged. If his father's friends found out about Halcón Rock, they could ruin everything. "What happened, exactly?"

"I found out Bonebrake planned to borrow Manny's truck. I planted a tracker on it and gave the info to my friends. I told them he was a researcher who might actually know what he was talking about, and I wanted to know if he found anything useful."

"And did he?" Matthew held his breath, waiting for the answer.

Sheriff Jameson shrugged. "I don't know. My intent was for them to follow him and let me know if he made a useful discovery or if he talked to anyone who might be useful. Instead, they followed him to the UNM library and tried to steal some articles he printed up off the Internet." Jameson rolled down the window, letting a blast of dry air in, and spat a wad of phlegm out onto the sun-baked asphalt. "There was a car chase, shots fired, and now Bonebrake is in the wind."

Matthew smiled. "That should scare him off."

Jameson slowly shook his head. "On the contrary, now he knows for sure we've got something big here."

"*I've* got something big." Matthew's cheeks warmed as soon as he uttered the words. Why did his father bring out the worst in him?

"Now, Bonebrake's in the wind, and if I've got the measure of the man, he's going to keep digging. We haven't seen the last of him."

Matthew considered this for a moment. "He's got to come back for his truck sometime. When he does, we could kill him and dump his body outside of town. Just another unsolved murder."

Jameson nodded. "Could be, but I don't think he'll prove that easy to kill."

"You don't think I can handle him?" Matthew had never killed a man before, but he'd taken down more than his share of self-styled tough guys in bars and clubs from Amarillo to Albuquerque. He was also an accomplished hunter. Taking aim and pulling a trigger was a simple matter.

Jameson didn't take his eyes off the road. "Open that folder and read what's inside."

Matthew picked up the manila folder that was tucked in the crack beside his seat and opened it up. Inside were a few printouts, all regarding Bonebrake: a few arrest records from long ago; some information on his service in the Navy; including commendations and awards; and another sheet simply titled "Rumors." The items on this list were too incredible to be taken seriously.

"Atlantis?" he read aloud. "Oak Island, the skunk ape,

alien contact. You expect me to believe this crap?"

"I expect you to understand what sort of person we're dealing with. That file paints a picture of something I've seldom encountered: a true believer who not only isn't crazy, but can handle himself. We need to tread carefully around this guy."

Matthew flipped back to the page that covered Bonebrake's naval service. A young, short-haired version of the big Cherokee smiled back at him. He had the sudden urge to slap that roguish grin right off the man's face. Maybe he'd get the chance.

"You have a plan?" he asked his father.

"Maybe we can turn his skills to our advantage. He has to come back for his own truck sometime. I've planted a tracker on it. Maybe we'll follow along and see where he leads us."

SIXTEEN

"I didn't know Los Alamos was part of the Department of Energy," Jessie said from the back seat of Amanda's Toyota 4 Runner as the blue sign reading *United States Department of Energy, Los Alamos National Laboratory* flashed past them. "I just figured it was military."

"That's a common misconception," Amanda said, keeping her eyes on the winding road. "The laboratory was founded during World War II as a home for the Manhattan Project, but nuclear is energy…" She didn't elaborate. They'd made the short, picturesque drive up from Santa Fe in a tense forty-five minutes. Bones had tried to break the silence several times with his trademark humor, but failed at every turn. He'd even resorted to pronouncing "butte" as "butt." No joy.

"And since the Manhattan Project, they've continued to conduct nuclear research?" Jessie asked.

"Much more than that. They focused on nuclear weaponry throughout the Cold War but have broadened their research since then. They've studied other forms of energy, done medical research on cancer and AIDS, non-nuclear threats, and response. Lots of stuff."

"If there's a zombie outbreak, there's a good chance it could start from in there." Bones nodded at the stretch of high, chain link fence topped with razor wire.

Amanda rolled her eyes.

"I'm serious. If a government agency is studying outbreaks and how to prevent them, you can bet they're also studying how to start them."

"Paranoid." Jessie kicked the back of his seat.

"Just realistic." He shook his head. "A lot of people believe they've conducted UFO research here."

"Why wouldn't they do that somewhere secret, like Area 51?"

"This place used to be secret, too. No one knew where it was. Just PO Box 1663, Santa Fe."

"It's sad that you know that, but you can't remember a girl's birthday," Amanda said.

"Look, chick, I remembered your birthday. I was stuck on a dive with…"

"…with Maddock," Amanda finished. "Have you two considered tying the knot? You're inseparable, and you bicker like an old married couple."

From the back seat, Jessie let out a tiny laugh.

"We've discussed it, but we can't agree who would get to lead when we slow dance," Bones deadpanned.

Amanda cracked a smile. "I can't believe I'm here with you. You have this way of creeping in like a fungus."

"Don't feel bad." Jessie reached over the seat and gave his shoulder a squeeze. "Fungi have many important uses: penicillin, dairy products…"

"You're not helping," Bones said. "Anyway, back to the UFOs. I…" He paused as Amanda turned onto the main drive leading to the laboratory. "What's up with this? I thought we were sneaking in?"

Amanda frowned. "Why would we sneak in? I arranged badges for us."

"Crap. I was really looking forward to sneaking in." He sat, muscles tensed, as they passed through security at the vehicle access control point. He was convinced something would go wrong. It was never this easy. However, they cleared security and drove to the Research Library. As Amanda parked the car in front of the two-story beige structure, Bones turned to her. "You still haven't told us what we're here for."

Amanda shook her head, slid out of the car, and slammed the door.

"Touchy," Bones whispered. He waited for Jessie, and then the two of them double-timed it to catch up with Amanda, who was already stepping through the broad, glass door.

They stopped at the front desk, where a wizened Hispanic woman with silver-streaked black hair and dark eyes greeted them with a frown.

"I have an appointment to meet with Mike Madden," Amanda said.

The receptionist gave a curt nod, picked up the phone, and dialed an extension.

"Who's he?" Bones asked. "Better not be competition."

"You listen to me." Amanda's words poured out in a

harsh whisper. "I have been working this guy for months, and you'd better not screw it up for me."

"Working him? Like a scam?"

"No. Yes. I mean…" She stamped her foot. "Just follow my lead. It would help if you acted like an idiot. That's how I've described you to him."

"Oh, so you told him about me. That means I've been on your mind." Bones grinned.

"Don't look so smug. I also told him you were a big guy except for where it counts most." Her eyes flitted downward for a second and Bones took a step back.

"Not cool. I'll play along, but don't blame me if he and I wind up at adjoining urinals."

"Cool it." Jessie took him by the hand. "I think that's him coming this way."

Madden was a man of around Bones' age with an athletic build and long, black hair. He greeted Amanda with a tight hug and a quick kiss on the lips.

"Check out the hair," Jessie said, glancing first at Madden's flowing locks and then at Bones' ponytail. "I think she has a type."

"No white guy is the same type as me," Bones said softly.

"I hate to break it to you, but 'big lug' is universal."

"Bones," Amanda said with sudden cheeriness, "I'd like you to meet Mike."

The two shook hands and traded appraising looks.

"I've heard a bit about you," Madden said, adopting a neutral tone. "I didn't realize you two were still in touch."

"It's a research thing," Amanda said quickly. "Bones and," she glanced at Jessie, "his girlfriend happen to be working on something related to a story I'm writing."

At the mention of "girlfriend", Madden's posture relaxed, and he flashed a warm smile. "That's great, although I'm bummed this visit isn't of a more personal nature." He winked at Amanda.

"Not this time, but we'll have to get together soon." Amanda lowered her voice. "Is there somewhere we can speak privately?"

Madden nodded. "We can go to my office. Come on."

As they strode through the quiet hallways, Bones looked

down at Jessie. "He's not that good-looking, is he?"

Jessie cast an appraising glance at Madden. "He's all right, but if he works here, he's probably a brain. I prefer them big and dumb." She flashed a wicked grin and took Bones' hand. "We're supposed to be a couple. Don't forget that."

Bones let out a sigh of resignation. "Somehow, I don't think you'll let me forget it."

Since they were in a library, he expected Madden's office to be stuffed with books, but instead, it was sleek and modern, with gray walls, glossy black furniture, and modern artwork. He took a seat on a small leather sofa, and Jessie squeezed in next to him, unnecessarily close, in his opinion, but that wasn't a bad thing.

Madden closed the door, and Amanda took a seat on his desk.

"Mike, I need to see the *Book of Bones*."

SEVENTEEN

"The *Book of* Bones, Mike." Amanda folded her arms and tapped her foot on the carpeted floor. "It's important."

A curtain of denial lowered over Madden's face. "There's no such thing."

"Yes, there is."

"Come on, Amanda." Madden forced a chuckle. "I know you've been writing about some odd stuff, but you act like you're beginning to believe it." He took two steps back and dropped into the leather chair behind his desk.

"I know it was here, Michael." Amanda's icy tone sent a chill down Bones' spine.

Madden lowered his head and stared resolutely at his desk.

"What is the *Book of Bones*? Did all my exes get together and write a slam book or something?" The joke did little to lighten the mood.

"It's a Native American artifact. Inside it are recorded myths, legends, and history of the Anasazi."

Jessie frowned. "The Anasazi? Aren't they a lost tribe?"

"Not exactly," Bones said. "Most likely they migrated and became the forerunners of the modern Puebloan peoples."

"Aren't they supposedly bad news? I read their name means something weird, like..." She narrowed her eyes, thinking.

"It means *Ancient People*," Madden supplied.

"That's the modern spin," Bones said. "People are trying to put a better face on the name. It's actually a Navajo word that translates as *Ancient Enemy*."

"So, what's our interest in this book?" Jessie asked.

"The *Book of Bones* includes stories of Anasazi contact with dwellers beneath the earth," Amanda began. "And not just the legends we're familiar with. Reportedly, it includes remarkable details, including the location of the path to the world beneath, and accounts of men who visited there."

Madden shook his head. "I'm telling you, Amanda, it's a bunch of crap. I've lost count of how many conspiracy theorists have come to me with this same story. If it's so real, why are there no records?"

"Because it's hidden here, suppressed because the contents are too... I don't know, sensational, dangerous."

"It's not here."

Amanda leaned forward, resting her palms on Madden's desk.

"I know it was here. Klaus Fuchs mentions it in his journal. He personally examined it and what he read scared him to death. So much so that he couldn't wait to get out of New Mexico."

"Who is this Fuchs guy?" Jessie asked.

"A spy," Bones growled. "He was a German socialist who worked on the Manhattan Project. During World War II and the early part of the Cold War he supplied secrets to the Russians."

"That part doesn't particularly interest me," Amanda said, her eyes still boring into Madden. "What interests me is the fact that he saw the *Book of Bones* in the secret library here at Los Alamos." She softened her tone. "Michael, someone tried to kill Bones and Jessie because of this."

"Then they ought to leave it alone." Madden's voice trembled.

The man was hiding something, and Bones knew it. For a moment he considered beating the secret out of Madden, but dismissed the idea. The guy was probably afraid of whoever it was that had come after Bones, and Bones wasn't willing to do what it would take to make himself seem the deadlier threat. Besides, if this *Book of Bones* really was hidden in a secret library, they'd need someone to get them in.

"Please," Jessie said. "It's too late for us to back off. They think we have information they want, and the only way we can end this is to get to the bottom of the mystery."

Madden wilted under the pleading gazes of the two attractive women.

"All right," he said, his shoulders sagging. "It does exist. But I wasn't lying when I said it isn't here."

"Where is it?" Amanda asked.

"Gone. Stolen."

"You have got to be freaking kidding me." Bones stood, closed his eyes, and pressed his hands to his temples, fighting back the urge to hit something or someone. *We can't catch a break.* He took a deep breath, let it out slowly, lowered his hands, and opened his eyes. "Any idea who took it?"

Madden shrugged. "I have my suspicions, but it's only that. I don't know anything for certain."

"Tell us," Amanda said.

"Several years back, the library brought in a researcher on contract. He was a little odd, but when you're surrounded by scientists and librarians, odd is normal. Anyway, not long after his contract ended, someone realized the book was gone. No one made the connection, but later I found out he's a conspiracy nut. He's all into the pyramids and ancient aliens and all that stuff. He would definitely be interested in the book. I passed my suspicions along to my supervisor, but Krueger had disappeared."

"Would he have had access to the secret library?" Amanda asked.

"No, but he worked with at least one person who does, and rumor has it, they were an item."

Bones couldn't believe his luck. All the tension drained from his body. He smiled and reached out to shake Madden's hand. "Mister Madden, you've been more help than you could possibly know."

He turned and strode out of the office, leaving a surprised-looking Madden behind and Amanda and Jessie hurrying to catch up.

"All right, Bones," Amanda said when they were back inside the car, "what's the deal? Do you know this Krueger?"

"We've met." Bones grinned, enjoying the chance to repay Amanda for her earlier secrecy.

"Do you know where he is now?" Jessie asked. "Madden said he disappeared."

"No, but I know someone who can reach out to him." A sudden thought struck him, and his glee evaporated.

"What's wrong?" Amada asked.

"I just realized something. If we want to get to Krueger, I'm going to have to call yet another ex-girlfriend."

EIGHTEEN

Bones sat on a picnic table overlooking the Rio Grande as it wended its way through the parched landscape of northern New Mexico. The Sangre de Cristo Mountains formed a spectacular backdrop, but he was in no mood to admire the scenery. Jessie and Amanda stood nearby, watching over him like a pair of guards. His stomach doing flip-flops, he took out his phone and made the call. He was pleasantly surprised when Avery Halsey answered on the first ring.

"If you're calling for bail money, try my brother." Aside from being one of Bones' exes, Avery was also the sister of his friend and business partner, Dane Maddock.

"And a good afternoon to you too. What makes you think I'm in jail?"

"Just messing with you. But seriously, I can't imagine anything good coming from you, Willis, and Matt together in Vegas."

"Well, I haven't actually gotten there yet. Engine trouble."

"Sorry, but I can't help you with that. I don't even know how to change oil."

"Actually, I need a different favor." The line went silent, and Bones thought he'd dropped the call. "Are you there?"

"Yes," she replied in monotone. *"Here I thought we might be getting to the point where I might get a friendly check-in call from you, but as usual, you want something from me."*

Bones heard a giggle and turned to see Jessie covering her mouth.

Stop eavesdropping, he mouthed.

"It's not like that. You know I wouldn't call unless it was serious business."

"You're off on another one of your adventures, aren't you? You can't even drive to Vegas without running afoul of someone along the way."

"I swear I don't do it on purpose."

"Sure." Sarcasm dripped from the single word. *"Is there a girl involved?"*

"Two, actually." Bones could have kicked himself. Why had he blurted that out?

Avery, for her part, actually found the admission amusing.

"Unsurprising, but refreshingly honest. Now, what is it you need? It better not be something that will get me in trouble with the boss." Avery was now part of the Myrmidon Squad, a CIA unit led by his old friend, Tam Broderick.

"I need to talk with Kirk Krueger. I know the Myrmidons helped him hide after…" He glanced at Amanda and Jessie, who both looked on with interest. "…after, you know." Krueger was a pseudo-scientist who specialized in alien contact with the Egyptians, but his base of esoteric knowledge was broad. Not too long ago he had aided Bones and Maddock in a search for the lost city of Atlantis, and the repercussions had forced him to go into hiding.

"I can't tell you where he is," Avery said.

"Can you just put me in touch with him. That's all I need."

A deep sigh on the other end of the line. *"All right I'll reach out to him and see if he's willing to talk with you."*

"That would be great. You sure it won't get you in trouble with Tam?"

"We helped Krueger hide, but he's still his own person. It's up to him to decide." She paused. *"Just to be safe, let's not tell anybody about this… aside from your new girlfriends, of course."*

"They're not my girlfriends," Bones said quickly, eliciting tiny laughs from Jessie, Amanda, and Avery.

"Mark my words. One of them will be by the end of this. And a couple months from now, she'll be your ex."

"That's cold."

They exchanged perfunctory goodbyes and hung up. Now the waiting began.

"So Avery's another ex-girlfriend?" Jessie asked.

Bones nodded.

"How'd you meet this one?" Amanda asked. "Were you out looking for the Loch Ness Monster or something?"

"Looking for treasure on Oak Island," he muttered.

Amanda barked a laugh. "You are truly a one-trick pony."

Jessie gaped at him. "So, all this treasure hunting and stuff is for real? You weren't just trying to impress me?"

"I'll tell you later," Bones said.

"I couldn't help but hear some of her end of the conversation," Amanda said.

"Because you were trying to hear," Bones retorted.

"Naturally. I am a reporter after all. Anyway, who is this brother she's talking about?"

Bones closed his eyes. "She's Maddock's sister."

Now it was Amanda's turn to gape. "Maddock has a sister? And you thought it would be a good idea to date her?"

"Well, Maddock's engaged to *my* sister."

Just then his phone vibrated, bringing the conversation to an end, though probably a temporary one. It was text message from Krueger. He read it, a grin spreading across his face.

"What is it?" Amanda asked.

"Road trip." He stood and headed for the car.

"You're awfully happy," Jessie said, falling into step with him. "Where are we going?"

"Somewhere I've always wanted to visit."

NINETEEN

Bones couldn't help but tap his foot on the floorboard and drum his fingers on the dashboard in nervous anticipation as the sign welcoming visitors to Roswell, New Mexico appeared up ahead. Beneath the words of welcome, a stylized Zia sun peeked up over mountain peaks, and below it, the slogan caught Bones' attention.

"Dairy capital of the Southwest," he read aloud. "That's not what I expected."

"Don't aliens like to give anal probes to cattle or something like that?" Jessie asked.

"They dissect them!" Bones said. "Have a little respect for the scientist from the other side of the galaxy, will you?"

"It's just the people who get probed," Amanda chimed in. "What is it with the probing, anyway? Are they all proctologists?"

"Screw you guys," Bones said. 'You're not going to kill my good mood. I've been wanting to visit here for years."

"You do seem pretty excited," Amanda said, keeping her eyes on the road. "I guess this is like Mecca to you."

"I don't know. Graceland is up there, too."

"Hey, check out the lampposts." Jessie pointed to one of the streetlamps that lined either side of the main street. "They're aliens."

Sure enough, the bulbous lamps were formed in the shape of alien heads and adorned with large, black eyes that peered at passing cars with sinister intent.

"So cool," Bones said.

"This guy we're going to meet, Krueger," Amanda began, "what can you tell us about him? Another UFO nut like you?"

Bones let the jibe pass. "Kirk Krueger. He helped me and Maddock out when we were looking for Atlantis."

"Atlantis?" Jessie interrupted. "Oh my God. Tell me you don't believe in that, too. It's a myth."

"We found it."

The simple declaration left the young woman gaping. "You're messing with me," she finally managed.

"Nope." Bones gave his head a single shake.

"This guy is full of secrets," Amanda said, glancing at Jessie in the rear-view mirror. "And he doles them out like candy. He loves the attention."

"That's not it at all. Some stuff is classified, other stuff would be dangerous for people to know. Besides, *'How'd you like to have a drink with the guy who found Noah's Ark?'* is a lousy pickup line."

"Noah's Ark," Jessie repeated, her voice flat. Her eyes flitted from Bones to Amanda, suspicion shining brightly. "I can't decide if the two of you are serious or just trying to make me feel stupid."

"I'm serious," Amanda said. "And he is too. At least, he is about this."

Jessie's shoulders sagged. "Who are you, anyway?"

Bones sighed. "Just a guy who can't stay out of trouble."

"Don't let him fool you," Amanda said. "He loves every second of it."

"Some of it's pretty cool, but it can get bad. It's definitely not for everyone."

"So, this Krueger guy," Jessie prompted.

"He's an expert on ancient mysteries, Egypt in particular, but he knows his stuff, especially as it relates to contact with extraterrestrials. He's been in hiding for a while now." Bones stopped there. To explain further would require a lot more back-filling than they had time for at the moment. "Those are the broad strokes. He's a good guy. If he had anything to do with the book's disappearance, he'll tell me."

Ten minutes later, they strolled up to the Roswell UFO Museum. The turquoise marquee shone brightly in the New Mexico sun, looking like a 1950s movie theater façade. They paid their admission fee and proceeded inside.

The museum was heavy on reprints of newspaper clippings and government documents, especially those relating to the famed Roswell Incident of 1947, in which the government allegedly recovered a crashed UFO. Bones had read most of it before, but he soon found himself drawn in by the sheer volume of information on UFO legends and conspiracies.

"Do we just wait?" Jessie whispered.

"He'll find us. I sort of stand out in a crowd."

They continued to browse the exhibits: equipment from the 1940s, dioramas of spaceship crashes, and models of aliens. Bones was enjoying the relative silence when a mechanical rumble filled the room, followed by a high pitched whine. His senses on alert, he looked around for the source of the sound and relaxed when his eyes fell on a group of aliens standing in front of a dark backdrop. Steam rose around them and above their heads, a scaled-down flying saucer rotated in midair.

"Cheesy," he muttered.

"True, but the visitors seem to like it." Bones glanced down to see a thin man of medium height smiling up at him. He hadn't met Krueger in person but recognized him from photographs. He'd dyed his hair brown, but his blue eyes and easy smile made him easy to recognize.

"You've got to be Bones."

"I don't really have much choice, do I?" They shook hands and Krueger ushered them into an office at the front of the building.

"You work here?" Bones said. "Won't that make you easier to find?"

"Hiding in plain sight. Our mutual friend, Tam, thought it a good idea. Besides, things have calmed down on the Dominion front. I don't feel like I'm in any real danger, but there's no harm in playing it safe."

At the mention of the Dominion, Jessie shot a sharp glance at Bones, but Amanda tapped her on the arm and mouthed, *I'll tell you later.*

"So, you're interested in the *Book of Bones*. I think I can..." He paused as the phone on the desk rang. "Excuse me." He answered the phone and frowned as the person on the other end of the line began to speak. As he listened, the lines in his brow deepened. When he hung up, his face was pale. "I don't know for sure, but I think we might have a problem. Some men are outside asking for you."

TWENTY

"Is there another way out of here?" As he spoke, Bones scanned the tiny office. No windows, no door other than that which led back into the museum.

Krueger shook his head. "Do you think it's the Dominion?"

"I don't know." The Dominion, a powerful extremist group with ties in business and government, had dogged Bones and Maddock's trail for years, and Krueger had found himself caught up in it. "I know they're pretty much broken in the U.S., but that doesn't mean they're gone. All I know is someone's been after us ever since Jessie and I started researching the incident at Halcón Rock."

Krueger blinked. "I can tell you a little something about that too, provided you can get us out of here." He moved to the door and peered out. "Two guys are coming this way. What do we do?"

Bones took another look around. His eyes wandered to the drop ceiling. "What's on the other side of this wall?"

"A storage room. Why?" Krueger looked up, his focus sharpened, and he nodded. "Good idea. I'll see what I can do to slow them down."

While Krueger locked the door and wrestled a heavy filing cabinet in front of it, Bones sprang into action. He leaped up onto Krueger's desk and beckoned to Jessie and Amanda to join him. He pushed aside a ceiling tile and boosted Jessie up. The athletic young woman clambered nimbly through the opening. Seconds later they heard a cry and a crash.

"I'm okay," came her muffled voice. "Fell onto a box of toilet paper."

A sharp knock at the door cut off Bones' reply.

"Yes? Can I help you?" Krueger was pushing a bookcase against the door, and the strain was evident in his voice.

"FBI. Open the door."

"Just a second, I'm…" Krueger clambered up onto the desk. "I'm looking at porn and need to put my pants back on."

"Excuse me?" the voice said.

"It was all I could think of," Krueger whispered as Bones boosted him up.

"Perfect," Bones chuckled.

Thunk! Something heavy hit the door. The men on the other side must have sensed Krueger was stalling.

Thunk! The door held.

Bones climbed up into the dark space above the drop ceiling, crawled forward, and dropped down into the storage room, where the others waited by the door.

"Where does the door lead?" he asked Krueger.

"Back into the…" Krueger's face went scarlet, and he cleared his throat. "Back into the museum."

"You've got to be freaking kidding me." Bones looked around the room for a weapon, anything that could get them out of this mess. His eyes took in the piles of boxes, the shelves, lined with cleaning supplies, the dirty sink, the mops, brooms, and buckets. He smiled as an idea came to him.

"Everybody grab a cloth, wet it and hold it over your face. Keep your eyes closed and wait by the door for me to tell you to run." While the others hurried to comply, he began gathering the materials he'd need.

"This had better work."

He hastily plugged the sink and began pouring in bleach. When the big sink was half-full, he opened several bottles of drain cleaner and added them to the mix. The reaction was immediate and overwhelming. His years of diving, as well as his general level of fitness, meant he could hold his breath much longer than the average man, and he'd need every second. He closed his eyes and kept pouring. His sinuses burned, and his skin began to tingle.

On the other side of the wall, a loud crash told him the men had broken through.

"Up there! They went through the ceiling!" Someone shouted.

Bones moved blindly toward the door, guided by the others' rasping coughs. His sharp ears picked out the sound of feet thumping atop Krueger's desk… a grunt as someone climbed up into the space above the ceiling… another set of feet on the desk.

"Go!" he rasped. "Hurry."

Krueger pushed the door open, and they all burst out into the museum, knocking aside startled patrons.

Back in the storage room, someone cried out in surprise. Bones grinned as the sound died into a choking cough.

"Gas leak!" His raw throat gave the words a raspy tone, but he got them out. "Everybody out! Call the fire department!"

As was the case in any such situation, the people didn't react immediately. They moved out of the way of the fleeing group. That was fine with Bones. They'd get out of there in a hurry once they realized what was going on, and in the meantime, they'd serve as an obstacle for their pursuers, who right now were probably finding it nearly impossible to see or breathe.

As they burst out into fresh air and dashed for the car, his vision began to clear, and his breathing eased. By the time they were heading out of town, their rear view mirror blessedly empty, he was feeling almost like himself again.

"What was that stuff? I look like I just smoked a bowl." Jessie pulled her eyelid back and leaned close to the mirror set in the visor.

"Chlorine gas. I went all World War II on them."

"You could have killed us," Amanda said.

"And what would they have done to us?" Bones asked.

"Fair point. So, what do we do next?"

"We find a quiet place to lie low, while Krueger here tells us all he knows about the *Book of Bones*."

TWENTY-ONE

"My God, will these flies give us a break?" Amanda swatted in futility at the cloud of biting flies that swarmed around her head. "They don't seem to be bothering you guys." She cast a baleful look at the others who stood nearby suppressing grins.

Krueger let out a puff of bluish smoke in her direction, temporarily scattering the insects. "They don't seem to like cigarettes. Have one?" He held out a battered pack of Marlboro Reds.

"I'll pass." Amanda waved the offer away but moved closer to the others.

"So that's the final resting place of Billy the Kid?" Bones nodded at the simple headstone at the end of the sidewalk. Enclosed in a black cage and set in front of a large cane cholla cactus, the roughly carved gravestone was the only feature in the enclosed space behind the Old Fort Sumner Museum.

"Maybe." Krueger shrugged and led the way toward the grave. "He's buried somewhere in here. Back then, they used wooden grave markers and a storm washed them all away shortly after he was buried. This marker is just a guess."

"Bummer," Bones said. "Why is it caged like that?"

"Thieves and vandals." They reached the gravesite and Krueger reached out to touch one of the bars. "The headstone was stolen more than once."

"Why?" Jessie asked. "It's not valuable, is it?"

"Who knows why? Same reason they have annual tombstone races here in town."

Amanda cocked her head. "Tombstone races? Is that what I think it is?"

Krueger chuckled. "If you're picturing people running around with eighty-pound slabs strapped to their backs, then yes. I can't explain it. Something about Billy the Kid brings out the crazy in people."

"It hasn't brought out too many crazies today." Bones' eyes swept the empty horizon before returning to the gravestone.

The marker memorialized not only Billy the Kid but two

others. At the top was inscribe the word "PALS." On the left was the name Tom O'Folliard, at the bottom Charlie Bowdre, and at the right, William Bonney.

"William H. Bonney. Alias, Billy the Kid. Died July, 18 something," Jessie read. "Looks like the vandals damaged the stone."

Krueger nodded.

"I have to say, I'm not too interested in sightseeing," Amanda said. "I want to know who the hell just came after us and how did they find us?"

"You know we had to get off the beaten path, and this place is as good as any," Bones said. Krueger had chosen the place somewhat at random. It lay northeast of Roswell in the direction of the interstate highway that would take them back to Albuquerque or Quemadura, depending on what they decided. He let out a heavy sigh that made him feel like a deflating tire, turned, and leaned against the metal cage. The sun had baked the bars, and he felt their warmth through his leather jacket. "I have a theory about how they found us."

"It's not because you stand out in a crowd," Jessie said, "because that wouldn't explain how quickly they were onto us."

Bones shook his head. "The incident at Halcón Rock has 'aliens' written all over it. If someone suspects, or knows, that I've been checking into something related to aliens, where's the one place in New Mexico I'm bound to show up sooner or later?"

Krueger nodded thoughtfully. "So they sent someone to keep an eye on the place. That's how they got ahead of you."

"I guess Tam will have to change your identity again," Bones said. "Sorry about that."

"Maybe not. They came looking for you, not for Kraig Klemmer. I should be okay for the moment."

"So, that's how they found us," Jessie said. "Any idea who they are?"

"I have an idea." Krueger flicked his cigarette butt out onto the dry brown dirt of the graveyard. Catching Amanda's disapproving glance, he hurried over, stubbed it out, and pocketed it. "Anyway, I can't prove they exist, but I've long heard rumors of a group called STAR."

"Let me guess," Bones said. "It stands for something

ridiculous."

"Steering Toward America's Roots."

"That's bad," Amanda said. "A simple acronym for simple minds, I suppose."

"If the rumors are true, they've got some bright and talented people among their ranks. Mostly ex-military, but they've got connections in other places as well, and their ranks are swelling."

"Sounds like the Dominion," Bones said.

Krueger nodded. "Somewhat, but their aims are not religious in nature. It's purely political. Limited government, with the exception of the military, limited taxes, again, except for defense spending. Basically, keep the borders secure on the outside, laissez-faire on the inside."

"I can't say I totally hate that idea," Bones said. "Then again, I've seen what powerful people inside the country already get away with. I don't know about giving them freer rein."

"But what do aliens have to do with that?" Amanda asked.

"Aliens?" Krueger asked. "Nothing. But alien technology, that's a different story." He slapped a fly that had landed on his neck. "Time for another smoke. Anyway," he continued as he lit up, "I told you the group is filled with ex-military. At least some of them have to know about the government cover-ups and have heard the stories of highly advanced alien tech. If they could get their hands on it…"

"Rebellion," Jessie finished. "Overthrow of the government."

"Perhaps," Krueger said, "but they'd settle for establishing their own small nation. Part of west Texas, southern New Mexico, which has a large population of expat Texans, pieces of Arizona and northern Mexico. They'd have oil and natural gas to export, and with sufficient alien tech they could defend their borders."

"Imagine the ripple effect that would have on the rest of the United States," Amanda said. "If a region managed to successfully break off from the rest of the country, that would embolden separatists all over to rebel. Even if they failed, it would be a bloodbath. How many innocent people would die? What would it do to our economy and our long-term stability?"

Bones grimaced. Amanda's words echoed his own

thoughts. Such an occurrence would send ripples not only across the nation but around the world. That couldn't happen.

"I think we all agree this STAR group sucks, but nothing you've told us has changed our goal. We need to get the *Book of Bones* before they do." Bones turned to Krueger. "We heard it disappeared around the time you worked at Los Alamos. Any idea where it is?"

Krueger took a long drag of his cigarette and let the smoke out in a long, slow exhale.

"Yes and no. I mean, I did steal it, after all."

TWENTY-TWO

Halcón Rock loomed in the distance, only a bump on the broad, empty horizon. Matthew grinned as it came into sight. Today was the day.

The Jeep dropped hard into a rut as he guided it across the rough dirt road. Matthew winced, thinking of what he had stored in the back seat. It was a reflex born of irrational thought. It wasn't like he was hauling nitroglycerine.

The road bent around a dense patch of piñon pine and juniper, and as he rounded it, he let his eyes and thoughts drift back to the rock, and the mysterious door beneath it. So distracted was he that he almost didn't notice the olive-colored transport vehicle barring the way.

"Damn!" He slammed on the brakes, and the jeep fishtailed as it skidded along the hard-packed dirt road. It came to rest in a dust cloud only feet from the side of the vehicle. "What the hell is…?" The words died in his throat as two men, clad in body armor and carrying automatic rifles, approached his jeep from either side. Mathew swallowed hard, took a deep breath, and rolled down the driver side window.

"What's going on here?" His voice sounded too high-pitched, almost shrill. He cleared his throat and continued. "I'm conducting research up at Halcón Rock."

"Site's closed." The speaker was a brick of a man—short and thick-bodied with a blocky build and a flat-topped haircut. The bright New Mexico sun shone off his aviator sunglasses and gleamed on the sweaty bald patch of tanned flesh on the crown of his head.

Matthew waited for the man to elaborate, but no further explanation was forthcoming.

"I've been working here for months. I assure you it's all legal. The sheriff is aware of the situation."

"Situation's changed." This time, the man on the passenger side spoke. He was of late middle years, with silver at his temples and deep cracks marring his weathered, coffee-and-cream complexion. Mischief danced in his whiskey colored eyes as he worked at a toothpick in the corner of his mouth.

Matthew wanted to step out of the jeep and smack the toothpick down the man's throat, but he was outnumbered and outgunned. His eyes took in the scene. The men wore desert camouflage clothing free of patches, insignias, or other identifying marks. Their vehicle was equally void of identification.

"Who are you guys? You're not Feds." Matthew wasn't certain of that statement, but his gut told him it was true.

"That's classified." Bald Spot cleared his throat and spat on the ground. "You need to get out of here, Sir."

"I have a right to be here." Matthew knew he was defeated. He supposed he could drive around the makeshift roadblock, but then what? They'd follow him and stop him climbing the rock. Hell, they might even shoot him.

Toothpick man rapped on the passenger window.

"What?" Matthew snapped.

The man pointed in the direction from which Matthew had come.

"Is that supposed to mean something? Use your words," Matthew said.

"Leave now, or we'll be forced to incarcerate you and impound your vehicle."

Matthew knew there was nothing left to say. He shifted into reverse and hit the gas, engulfing the two men in a thick fog of dust. Neither of them flinched. He yanked the wheel hard to the left and hit the brakes. The jeep skidded off the road and came to a halt. Matthew shifted into drive, floored it again, and tore away down the road. As he drove away, he gave the men the one figure salute for good measure.

"Son of a…" He pounded his fist on the dashboard. Who the hell were these guys, and how had they found out about Halcón Rock? Were they friends of his dad? Surely his father would have warned him of potential interference. That left Bonebrake.

According to his father, the Cherokee's biography was as full of holes as Swiss cheese, but he had military and government connections. Matthew's thoughts raced. Bits and pieces of information sorted themselves and began to fall into some semblance of order.

"Sure, you just *happened* to break down in Quemadura," he

muttered. "You went jogging and just *happened* to run straight to Halcón Rock. And you just *happened* to chat up my girlfriend." That sealed it. Bonebrake was behind this, and Matthew needed to find out exactly what the man knew, and Matthew knew where to start.

The sound of a vehicle rumbling up her dirt driveway roused Mari from fitful sleep. She rolled over and looked at the clock on her bedside table. It was late morning. She hadn't intended to sleep in, but it was her day off, so why not? Squinting against the bright light, she turned to see who was coming. Her heart sank when she recognized Matthew's jeep. He was the last person she wanted to see.

She hastily threw back the covers and climbed out of bed. The tile floor felt cold under her bare feet, but the air inside her tiny bedroom was already warm and heading toward hot. She could open the windows and catch a breeze, but that would mean a house coated in dust before too long. She longed for an air conditioned home, but she couldn't afford even a tiny window unit.

She hurriedly tugged on a pair of sweatpants and a loose-fitting shirt and tousled her hair for good measure. Maybe if she convinced Matthew she was sick, he'd leave. Not for the first time, she chided herself for lacking the courage to end it with him. He just never took no for an answer. The solution was to get out of this place, but where could she go? She had no money, an incomplete education, and no job skills beyond waitressing. She was stuck.

Three sharp knocks and the front door squeaked open. Mari winced at the sound of heavy footfalls covering the few steps from the front door to her bedroom. She hopped back onto the bed, leaned back against the headboard, and closed her eyes.

"Mari?" Matthew opened the door. "What's your problem?"

"Migraine," she groaned. "It kept me up all night."

Matthew snorted. "I'll bet you didn't have a migraine when you were talking to your new *friend*."

Mari froze. She covered the reaction by slowly raising her hands to her head and massaging her temples. "What are you talking about?"

"How much time have you spent in Bonebrake's hotel room?"

"I went there to tell him to leave you…" The words were out before she could stop them, and she hadn't finished her sentence when Matthew grabbed her by the wrists and hauled her to her feet.

"I knew it! What did you tell him?" Matthew yanked her up so their noses were almost touching.

Mari stood, trembling, on her tiptoes. She could see every blemish in his scarlet face, feel his hot breath. She tried to push away, but he shook her with such force that a sharp pain shot up her neck. The meager resistance she'd mustered now melted away. She tried a softer approach.

"Matthew, you can't think I like that man."

"You admit to being in his hotel room?"

"Only to tell him to stay away from Halcón Rock," she said in a rush.

"What else did you tell him about the rock?"

"Nothing at all. Just to stay away." She gazed into his wide eyes, wondering what would happen next.

Matthew's shoulders sagged, and he relaxed his grip on her.

"I wish I could believe you." He turned, pushed the bedroom door closed, and turned back to face her. "But I need to make sure you're not lying."

TWENTY-THREE

"You stole the book?" Bones gaped at Krueger. Why hadn't the man said something before now? "So you have it?"

Krueger shook his head. "Not exactly."

"You are making zero sense, you know that?" Amanda folded her arms and scowled.

"I know, I know." Krueger began to pace. "I stole the book from Los Alamos, but it's a fake. A clever one, to be sure, but it's not the genuine article."

"How can you be sure?" Bones asked.

"Lots of reasons." Krueger stubbed his cigarette out, pocketed it, and immediately lit another. "I first grew suspicious when I began translating it. Things that should have been there weren't."

"Like what?" The frown hadn't left Amanda's face.

"There were no stories about the Ant People. Nothing that even hinted at the existence of underground dwellers, or even sky people, for that matter. There was nothing but the usual legends."

"Maybe that's all there ever was," Jessie offered. "I mean, you didn't see the original."

"No, but Klaus Fuchs did, and there was a lot in that book that wasn't in my copy. Anyway, I took it to an expert who knows how to keep a secret, and he confirmed the forgery." Krueger sighed. "Someone went to a lot of trouble."

"Any idea who?" Bones asked.

Krueger nodded. "I'm almost one hundred percent certain I know who has it. And I'm afraid I know what he's done with it."

Bones didn't like the sound of that. "I'm afraid to ask."

"I think Gregory Glade paid someone to steal it for him."

Amanda rolled her eyes and let out a low groan.

"The name sounds familiar, but I can't place it," Bones said.

"He's that crazy millionaire who hid the treasure," Jessie said. "Once a month he gives a new clue to its location. One of my friends thinks he knows where it is. He wants me to help him search for it over spring break."

Now Bones remembered. Gregory Glade was an odd one, no question about that. He'd built a small, but luxurious home inside a cave somewhere in the Sangre de Cristo Mountains. He was rarely seen in public, save for his annual appearance at opening day for the indoor football team of which he was the sole owner. What's more, his name had been associated with black market antiquities deals, though that was merely a rumor.

"And you think he hid the *Book of Bones* along with the treasure?"

Krueger nodded. "The Feds searched his home and his holdings and found no illegal artifacts. Not one week later, he announced his treasure hunt."

"Maybe the treasure consists of all the illegal artifacts he's collected," Amanda mused. "If anyone ever finds it, he's screwed."

"Only if the finder goes public," Bones said.

"And only if they find it before he dies," Jessie added.

"What makes you think Glade has it? Or had it?" Bones said to Krueger.

Krueger was about to speak, but a sudden frown creased his brow. "Let's get out of here. I see some actual tourists coming."

Bones snapped his head around, senses on high alert. He relaxed when he saw an elderly couple approaching. He stepped off the sidewalk to give them room to pass, and the others followed suit.

"Thank you, young fellow." The man paused and frowned. "Did anybody ever tell you you're one damn big Indian?"

"Only every girl who sees me naked." Bones winked.

The old man let out a loud cackle and his wife covered her mouth, her blue eyes dancing with delight.

"Don't believe him," Amanda called back over her shoulder as the group headed for the parking lot. "I've seen him naked, and he's using all his length elsewhere."

Now everyone laughed. Everyone except Bones.

"Don't make me prove you wrong out here in public," he said.

"Please. Maddock told me the shrinkage story."

"It was cold water. Really cold," Bones protested over a new wave of laughter. "Ask him about the time I fished him out of the drink off Wrangel Island. I guarantee you he was… ah, forget it."

Back in the car, Krueger resumed his explanation. "Once I identified my book as a forgery, I started searching for the real book. I found a few clues. About ten years ago there was a scientist at the lab who shared some of my interests if you know what I mean."

"Little green men?" Amanda quipped.

"Among other things. Anyway, he kept it quiet because you know how the scientific community rejects anything too different, but we ran in some of the same circles, so I was aware of his leanings. He quit Los Alamos unexpectedly and moved to Crested Butte, Colorado. He bought a five million dollar home there. Now he spends his days skiing and his evenings writing about aliens."

"He definitely wouldn't make that kind of money at the lab," Jessie said.

"He sold something valuable to someone," Krueger said. "Less than a month after this man leaves the lab, Glade suddenly becomes a true believer in the so-called 'world beneath.' He hops on message boards and assures people he knows it's true, though he won't say how he knows. He even grants an interview where he says the same thing."

"It's thin," Amanda said. "You have anything else?"

"A picture. Glade allowed the interviewer to snap a single photograph inside his home. In the background, you can see what I believe is the *Book of Bones*. It's only the corner, mind you, but it's identical to my copy."

Amanda pursed her lips and frowned. Her eyes remained locked on the road ahead, but she was clearly deep in thought. "If anyone is crazy enough and rich enough to make a copy of the book and have it switched out for the original, it's Glade."

"Even if he did include the book with the treasure, do you think he made a copy? Took photos? I've got a friend who could hack his network for us." Bones was already reaching for his phone to call Jimmy Letson, a former Navy comrade and an accomplished hacker.

"He has no network. He goes to a coffeehouse to get

online." Krueger sighed. "I even tried bribing the reporter to tell me where Glade's home is, but he was taken there in a panel van. He said it was like being abducted. He did, however, confirm seeing something that might have been the book. He didn't get a good look at it, but what he saw fits the description."

"What does it look like?" Jessie asked.

"It's basically a stack of tanned, scraped hides with fine writing burned into both sides. It's wrapped in bones bound together with strips of hide, almost like a breastplate a warrior would have worn into battle."

"I thought the Ancestral Puebloans didn't have a written language," Bones said.

"They didn't. The stories were passed down orally and recorded much later. They're written in an odd mix of Spanish, phonetic representations of Tewah, a Puebloan language, and pictures and symbols. It was probably written by someone educated by a Spanish missionary."

Bones stared out at the hot, dry landscape whizzing past them in a brown blur, and considered their options. "Assuming you're right about the book, option one is to comb the Sangre de Cristos looking for Glade's home, hope we can get past whatever security he's put in place, and hope he made a copy of the book, and hope we can find that copy."

"What's option two?" Amanda asked.

"Find the treasure."

"I was afraid you were going to say that." She shook her head. "Do you know how many people have tried and failed? At least one person has died in the hunt."

"I do have experience with this sort of thing," Bones said.

"Don't forget about my friend," Jessie said. "We can ask…" She broke off as her phone rang. She answered, and after a brief, quiet conversation, hung up.

"That was Manny. Your truck is ready."

"Good. I've missed my Ram." He noticed her frown. "What's up?"

"He said Mari is in the hospital, and she's in bad shape."

TWENTY-FOUR

From his hiding place behind an abandoned store, Sheriff Craig Jameson watched the blue Dodge Ram pull slowly out of the parking lot of Miguel's Automotive and Pawn. Cupping the screen of his cellphone to hide the glow, he checked the open app. Sure enough, a tiny red dot tracked the movement of the pickup truck as it headed down the road. Bonebrake thought himself clever, sneaking out in the middle of the night, but now Jameson could track the man wherever he went. And so could Jameson's friends.

Smiling, he tucked the phone into his pocket and headed in the opposite direction to the spot where he'd parked his patrol car. No need to follow Bonebrake just yet. If the man went somewhere interesting, Jameson would pass the word through the proper channels. Hopefully, the troublesome Indian would continue on his way and never set foot in Quemadura again.

When he reached his parked patrol car, he found Matthew waiting for him. The back of Jameson's neck prickled and he took a few calming breaths before approaching his son. If the boy, and in many ways that's what Matthew still was, kept screwing up, Jameson would be forced to deal with it. He loved his son, but at some point, his hands would be tied.

"Did you let him go?" Matthew said when his father came within earshot.

"The man who put Mari in the hospital? I'm afraid I did."

That got a reaction. Matthew flinched, and his eyes drifted toward the ground. "She had an accident."

"So I wrote in my report." Jameson sat down on the hood of his squad car and motioned for Matthew to join him. He gritted his teeth, biting down a rebuke, as his son sulked over to his side. The car dipped as Matthew let his bulk drop onto the bumper. He sat there, arms folded, staring down the empty street.

"I meant Bonebrake," Matthew said. "You just let him leave?"

"I told you I planted a tracker on his pickup. I can get to him any time I like."

"I need that tracking information," Matthew said. "I've got business with him."

Jameson shook his head. "I don't want to talk about Bonebrake." He took a deep breath. "I want you to know, that's the last time I'll sweep something under the rug for you."

Matthew humphed. "I don't know what you're…"

"Stop it!" Jameson turned to his son, who continued to stare into the distance. "I don't care how you fix this problem, but fix it you will. You want some in-patient treatment somewhere? I'll pay for it. You want to leave town and start over somewhere else? I'll pay for that too. But you will leave that girl alone, and you won't put your hands on a woman ever again. However you need to do it, get your shit together."

"I can't leave here until I finish what I've started."

"You can finish your book anywhere," Jameson said.

"You know what I mean. The rock is the key. I need to find out what's behind that door."

"And you thought blowing it with a big mess of C-4 was the answer?" Jameson raised an eyebrow.

"How did you…" Matthew's shoulders sagged. "I couldn't get it open, so I figured I had to go around it."

"Do you even know how many things are wrong with that idea? How many reasons it probably wouldn't work? Not to mention you have no training with explosives."

"You have no respect for me." Matthew sprang to his feet and began to pace. "What if Bonebrake's men get there before me?"

"Bonebrake's men? Out at the rock? Those are my…acquaintances."

Matthew stopped dead in his tracks and slowly turned to face his father. "I can't believe you did that. I considered the possibility, but I never thought you'd betray me like that."

"You don't understand what's at stake here." Jameson rose to his feet. "Once Bonebrake found the door, it was only a matter of time before the secret got out. And if those men learned that I'd been hiding something this important from them…"

"So you just handed it over to them?" Matthew asked.

"All they know is a man with suspicious government connections, and a history of meddling in things of this nature has been poking around. They know the Halcón Rock legend, but that's it. They don't know anything else and if you want it to stay that way, keep your head down and your mouth shut. They've got the place cordoned off as a precaution, but as far as I know, they're not actively searching for a path to…you know."

"So you believe it leads to the world beneath?" Matthew asked.

Jameson shrugged. "It makes as much sense as anything else. The truth, whatever it turns out to be, will be stranger than fiction, as they say."

"That's just it," Matthew pleaded. "I want to know what the truth is. Whoever built that door is hiding something. What is it?"

"There's another possibility." Jameson turned his eyes to the full moon and tried to ignore the shiver running down his spine. "What if that door was built to keep something from getting out?"

TWENTY-FIVE

"I freaking hate hospitals." Bones shrugged his leather jacket up as if it could shield him from the antiseptic smell and the underlying current of fear that pervaded the place.

"Why?" Jessie glanced up at him, a bemused frown painting her face.

"You don't come here unless you're sick or dying. Not my kind of place."

"People come here to get better. It's a place of healing." She reached out and took his hand. "And don't forget, some people come here to have babies. You know, to bring new life into the world?"

"That's an entirely different type of horror."

Jessie giggled and leaned her head against his shoulder. It was only for an instant and then she drew away, but the sense of familiarity, even affection, was palpable. She stole another glance at him, the too-bright lights reflected in her dark eyes. Neither of them spoke, nor did either let go of the other's hand.

"I'm not sure I should be here," Bones said. "I barely know Mari."

"She asked to see you," Jessie said. "And Manny's there. Maybe you can talk him out of doing something crazy to Matthew."

"Not likely." The very mention of Matthew's name sent waves of rage through Bones. He craved a confrontation with the arrogant man, the opportunity to lay hands on the coward."

"Ouch. You're crushing my hand."

"Sorry." Bones loosened his grip.

"That's better." Jessie suddenly halted. "Listen to me. We don't know for certain Matthew did this to her."

Bones looked down at the young woman. "You don't believe that, do you?"

Jessie stared hard into his eyes. "It doesn't matter what either of us believe. He's the sheriff's son. You'd end up in prison."

"Not if I did it right."

"You can't mean that." Jessie released his hand, reached up, and took his face in her hands. "You and I both know that nothing is going to change for Mari until she changes. If it's not Matthew, it'll be another guy just like him. The best thing we can do for her is help her do that."

"That's pretty much what Amanda said before you and I left the waiting room."

"Well, she's right, and so am I."

As he looked into Jessie's eyes and considered her words, Bones was once again forced to revise his opinion of her. "You know, when I met you, I thought you were just some sorority bimbo."

"What do you think now?"

"Still figuring you out. I'll let you know." He winked.

They entered Mari's room without knocking. She was sitting up in her bed, watching a game show on mute. She smiled when she saw Bones.

"You look good." He meant it. He'd expected her to be battered and bruised, but save the faintest trace of the bruised eye he'd noticed at their first meeting, her face was free of blemish.

"It's my ribs," she said. "I took a bad spill."

Bones didn't bother to contradict her. He could tell by the look in her eyes she knew he didn't believe her lie.

He squeezed himself into the chair in the corner of the room while Jessie took a seat on the side of the bed. They made small talk for a few minutes before Mari asked to speak to Bones alone. Jessie gave her friend a peck on the forehead, flashed a warning look at Bones, and slipped out of the room.

"Please don't do anything to him," Mari said as soon as the door closed.

"To who?"

"You know who—Matthew. And it's 'to whom', by the way."

"So you admit he's the one who did this to you?" Bones kept his voice calm, though he felt his ire rising.

Mari shook her head. "I didn't say that. I just know that you think he did it."

They sat in silence for a moment.

"Is that it, or is there more?"

Mari hesitated. "I think there's a way you can get back at Matthew without going to prison."

"I'm listening."

"Figure out the mystery of Halcón Rock before he does. He considers it his life's work. You could beat him up, but cuts and bruises will heal. If you can solve the mystery, it'll eat at him for the rest of his life."

"Can't I do both?"

"Not if you want what I have."

"And what is that?"

"Not until you promise you won't go after Matthew."

Bones wanted to argue with her, to ask her why she was protecting the dirtbag, but he knew it was never that simple in this kind of relationship. His eyes bored into hers, but her determination didn't waver.

"All right," he said. "I promise I won't go after him. But if he should come after me, I'm going to defend myself."

Mari nodded. "I guess that's the most I can hope for." She paused, her eyes searching the room. Finally, she again met Bones' eye. "All this time I made excuses for Matthew because I thought that, deep down, he truly loved me. Yesterday I found out it was all a lie."

"I'm sorry this is what it took to make you realize that, but I'm glad you did. This kind of relationship isn't love." He thought about the things Amanda and Jessie had said to him, and hastily added, "You should be proud of yourself for figuring that out. Some people never do."

A single tear trickled from the corner of Mari's eye. "You might want to save your accolades. The reason I realized it isn't what you think."

"What is it, then?"

"He told me he'd been waiting and waiting and he wasn't going to wait anymore. Then he asked 'Where is it?' over and over again."

"Where is what?" Bones asked.

"My father was a researcher who was into all the stuff Matthew is studying. Aliens, underworld dwellers, lost treasures, even the chupacabra."

"I know a little something about that last one."

Mari smirked. "Sure you do. Anyway, Papi kept his work

quiet. In such a small town, he was afraid his work would reflect badly on me, so he kept it to himself. When he died, I hid it all away. I thought no one else knew, but somehow Matthew found out about it. Turns out, that's the only reason he pretended to be interested in me. When I think about what I put up with from him and all the while, he just wanted Papi's research. God, I'm such an idiot."

"Don't do that to yourself. We're all stupid for love sometimes."

"I suppose. I guess I should give him credit for his patience. He stuck with me for a long time."

"Do you think your father knew something about Halcón Rock?"

"Matthew certainly thought so. I'm not sure what's in his research, but he always claimed to know more than anyone else in town. His big thing was the Gregory Glade treasure. He was pretty sure he had solved that one."

Bones perked up at the mention of the treasure. "Seriously?"

Mari forced a small, sad smile and turned to gaze out the window. "He was on his way to the spot where he swore the treasure was hidden when he ran off the road and was killed."

"I'm sorry," Bones said. "I never had a father, but I know how it feels to lose people you care about. It's happened to me more times than I care to count."

"Thanks."

"If you're willing to share his research with me, I think it could help more than you know."

"It's yours if you want it. It's brought me nothing but heartbreak." Her gaze softened as if she were staring at something only she could see.

"Is that why you never tried to find the treasure yourself?"

Mari laughed. "Partly, but could you imagine me hunting treasure? I wouldn't know where to begin. I'm a waitress. That's all I'll ever be."

"What if I told you that's not true?"

"I'd say you're sweet. A liar, but sweet."

Bones leaned forward, all business. "Mari, look at me. I need you to understand something. This isn't just a race between me and Matthew. There's someone else involved—

someone dangerous."

"More dangerous than Matthew and the sheriff?"

"Yes. They've already tried to kill me once. I don't know who they are or what kind of resources they have at their disposal, but they caught up to me again after I thought I'd shaken them."

"I'm sure you can handle it."

"It's not me I'm worried about. I don't know if Matthew is connected to the people who are after me, but if he knows your secret, we have to assume it's going to get out. If they find out about it…"

For the first time, Mari looked frightened. "What do I do?"

"Let me move you to somewhere safe until this blows over." He stood, moved to her bedside, and took her hand. "I know people who can help you start over for real. I'm talking an ironclad new identity, maybe even set you up with a new job and a new life. If you're willing."

Mari's lower lip trembled. "Why would you do that for me?"

"It's not easy to explain, but mostly because it's the right thing to do. You've put up with enough crap in your life. It's time you got a break."

"All right, I'll do it. The doctor says they'll release me tomorrow morning."

"Great. You can stay with a friend of mine while I make the arrangements." He'd have to set her up at Amanda's place. She'd give him a hard time about it, but she wouldn't say no to someone in Mari's plight. "If I'm not here when you're released, someone will be."

Mari gave his hand a squeeze. "I'd hug you, but I'm afraid it would hurt my ribs."

"That's okay," he chuckled. "So, is your dad's research hidden somewhere in your house?"

"No. I hid it at one of Papi's favorite places. You shouldn't have any problem finding it, but you'll have to be careful."

Bones grinned. "Chick, that's the story of my life."

TWENTY-SIX

"This looks like the place." Bones pulled his truck over to the side of the dirt road and cut the engine. All around, the rich, brown hills, dotted with patches of green, shone beneath the clear, cornflower blue sky. It was hard to believe that only a twenty-minute drive from Albuquerque could put them in a spot that felt like the middle of nowhere.

"I'll admit I was a bit skeptical of Mari's directions." Jessie held up the paper on which Bones had jotted some notes. "Bear right at the railroad tracks, turn left at the railroad storage area, head toward the landfill until you see the gate on your left." She chuckled.

"Sounds like something out of a bad comedy movie," Bones agreed. "Well, let's get moving. She said it should be easy to find where she hid the box, but who knows?"

They stepped out into the warm day. A gentle breeze stirred the dust that seemed to pervade this part of New Mexico.

"It's so dry here," Jessie said. "One of these days I want to move somewhere that actually has water."

"I like it," Bones said. "It's not Key West, but it's not bad in its way."

"You'll have to show me Key West sometime."

Bones smiled but didn't meet Jessie's eye. She wasn't quite hitting on him, but she was definitely testing the waters, and he wasn't ready to deal with that just yet. As they headed for the gate, he wondered what his problem was. When had he ever passed up an opening, even a small one? The girl was cute, smart, clever, capable, if inexperienced. Normally he'd be all over her. What made this different?

On the opposite side of the road, a double gate barred the way. To its left, a narrow stile afforded passage beyond the fence line.

"So, what's the deal with you and Amanda?" Jessie asked as they passed through, Bones ducking beneath the bar overhead.

"Nothing for a long time. I guess we're friends…maybe."

"I thought I sensed some kind of spark between the two of you." Jessie's face reddened as she spoke.

"Friction causes sparks." Bones was proud of that turn of phrase. Too bad his friends weren't around to hear it. "She's got her reasons to be pissed off at me, but that's all there is."

"Mari seems to like you."

The girl was definitely fishing.

"I'm no expert, but I think Mari needs to stay away from men for a long time. She's got some things she needs to fix in her own life." Bones grimaced. He didn't need this distraction right now. Wait. What was he thinking? When did he ever consider a hot girl, much less three of them, a distraction? Who was he? Maddock? "Look, I grew up a broke, troublemaking Indian kid in the middle of redneck heaven, so I know how it feels to be treated like you're nothing. That's why I feel bad for Mari. If I can help her out, cool, but I'm the last guy who's going to tend to the bird with the broken wing, or whatever they call it."

"You like the independent type?" Jessie said.

"I like the type who doesn't expect you to call her back." It was harsh, and a wave of guilt hit him like a slap the instant he'd said it, but it was for the best. He needed to focus, and this intrusion from his…feminine side, or whatever the hell it was, was unwelcome.

"Sure you do." Jessie smirked, then held up the paper again. "Two miles that way." She pointed to a rutted, overgrown dirt track that led off to the right. Beyond it, a solitary mountain loomed in the distance. "You take the lead, tough guy."

A short, silent walk later across parched ground strewn with thistles and sage, they came to a gate, actually more of an opening in a barbed wire fence, and passed through. They followed the fence line until they spotted the first marker stone: a black rock with an arrow scratched in the surface. After another brief walk, they came to their destination.

"I've wanted to see this for a long time," Bones said. "The Los Lunas Decalogue Stone."

Located near the base of Hidden Mountain near Los Lunas, the Los Lunas Decalogue Stone, or Commandment Rock was a controversial artifact— a boulder engraved with a

THE BOOK OF BONES | 123

truncated version of the Ten Commandments, it was written in what some called Paleo-Hebrew, a form of writing much like Phoenician, and dated by experts to 500 BCE.

"The natives call this place The Cliff of Strange Writings," Jessie said, "not only because of this stone, but because of what's at the top of the mountain." She examined the large stone. Nestled against the cliff face atop a pile of smaller stones, the eighty-ton boulder stood at a forty-five-degree angle, the top of it reaching just above her head.

Bones moved in for a closer look. The lines of white text were carved deeply, with a subtle geometric precision to the lines, the top of which had been defaced by vandals years before. Its surface was shaded by the gray-green foliage of a tamarisk tree— the very same type of tree planted by Abraham at Beersheba at a site known to this day as Abraham's Well. Bones had done his share of reading about this, and similar "pseudo-archaeological" finds, like the Kensington Runestone, the Bat Creek Tablet, and the Newark Holy Stones, and had brushed up on it after talking with Mari. While many considered it an obvious forgery, perhaps even a hoax perpetrated by two University of New Mexico students, a number of researchers believed it to be a genuine Pre-Columbian artifact.

"What exactly does it say?" Jessie asked.

Bones took out his phone and opened the browser where he'd bookmarked some articles about the site, and began to read.

"I am Jehovah your God who has taken you out of the land of Egypt, from the house of slaves. There must be no other gods before my face. You must not make any idol. You must not take the name of Jehovah in vain. Remember the Sabbath day and keep it holy. Honor your father and your mother so that your days may be long in the land that Jehovah your God has given to you. You must not murder. You must not commit adultery. You must not steal. You must not give a false witness against your neighbor. You must not desire the wife of your neighbor nor anything that is his."

"Okay, so literally a shortened version of the Ten Commandments. I guess I was expecting a little something extra thrown in there."

"It's still pretty cool," Bones said. "My kind of stuff." He glanced up toward the top of the mountain. "I guess we'd better get a move on. From what I understand, this isn't half as cool as what's waiting for us up there."

TWENTY-SEVEN

They paused at the top of the mountain to take in the scenery. To the northeast, the sharp outline of the Sandias loomed dark on the horizon. As he turned toward the west, the land flattened out, and Bones imagined he could almost see Arizona across the broad desert expanse. For a moment, he forgot everything that had happened over the past few days and simply took in the grandeur.

The moment passed all to quickly and he returned to full alertness when Jessie elbowed him in the ribs. "You still with me?"

"Just taking it all in."

Jessie smiled and gave his hand a quick squeeze. "I knew it. Within that coarse exterior lies the soul of a poet."

"Yeah." Bones let out a little chuckle. "There once was a girl from Nantucket…"

"I've never heard that one," Jessie said. "Was that Henry David Thoreau?"

"More like Henry David Bathroomwall." Bones looked around. "So, what all is up here?"

"According to Mari's directions, we first have to find the…" She furrowed her brow and stared intently at a small notepad. "The kettle's coat?" She cocked her head, bemused. Bones couldn't help but notice how cute she looked at that moment.

"What's that again?"

"She says it's like, Aztec, or something."

"Could she have possibly said Quetzalcoatl?" Bones asked.

"That's it. You're brilliant." Jessie punched him on the shoulder. "Sorry. I didn't hurt you, did I?"

Bones didn't dignify the question. Instead, he began the search for something that resembled the feathered serpent of Mesoamerican lore. After a brief search, the only thing they had spotted that even vaguely fit the bill was a pictograph that looked more like an inchworm from a children's storybook than the ancient deity.

"Could this be it?" he asked.

"She did say it looked kind of like a snake or a worm.

What is it supposed to look like?"

"Uglier, angrier, more feathered." He knelt down for a closer look. "I suppose some of these lines could signify feathers." He ran his finger along the line of the twisting creature, being careful not to actually touch it. "I still say it's an inchworm, but for now, let's say it's Quetzalcoatl. What's next?"

Jessie consulted their notes. "Now we find the tortoise."

They scoured the mountaintop, inspecting the various ruins that comprised what Jessie said might have once been an ancient settlement.

"Some researchers have identified these ruins as dwellings and an animal enclosure. Some say it served the purpose of defense and was used as an observation post."

"All I know is, I don't see a single stone or structure that's shaped like a tortoise." He looked around, and his eyes fell on a dark stone covered in tiny images. "Let's take another look at the star map."

The so-called "star map" depicted the zodiac constellations Sagittarius, Scorpio, Libra, and Virgo, as well as several other constellations. Based on the positions of the various stars, and the location of an image some believed to be a representation of a total solar eclipse, combined with the orientation of the stone, it was theorized that this map dated back to the year 107 BCE.

"It's not shaped like a tortoise," Jessie mused.

"No, but maybe there's something hidden in the star patterns. I was so focused on the shape of the rocks that I might have missed something."

"I thought you said you've solved a bunch of mysteries."

"I work with a partner. I'm brute force; he's fine detail."

"That Maddock guy?" Jessie asked, skirting a stone carved with a Hebrew phrase that, according to their notes, translated to, *Jehovah our Mighty One.* "Maybe you should give him a call. Get us some backup."

"Not happening. He's on a cruise with my sister. Even if I could reach him, he couldn't get back, and my sister wouldn't let him."

Jessie pursed her lips. "Won't let him?"

"If you knew my sister, you'd understand." Seeing the

doubt in her eyes, he took out his cellphone and saw that he had one bar of service. "Check this out." He called Maddock's number and switched to speaker phone. A long silence ensued, followed by two crackly rings, and then Angel's voice came on the line.

"He's on vacation, assclown."

"Angel, I need…" The call ended. Bones smiled at Jessie. "If I call again, she'll block my number. Guaranteed."

"Loving family you've got there."

"It works for us. I'm not exactly brother of the year."

Jessie let it drop as they reached the star map. "I don't see a tortoise."

"Wait a minute." Bones slowly circled the stone. "I'm an idiot. Look at it from this angle."

Jessie moved within a few paces of him and halted. "You're standing in a patch of yucca."

"Which is why we didn't see it before. Look there."

"Jerry is a tortoise?"

In the middle of the stone, a person had carved his name. Bones grimaced. "Don't you love people who deface historical sites? Somebody ought to slap him and the person who raised him."

Jessie flashed a sly grin. "So, your parents are to blame for your misdeeds."

"Fair point. Comment withdrawn. At least, the last part. But look at the 'y' in 'Jerry' and then let your eyes move straight up from there. See it?" He pointed to a white circle with six short, thick lines extending from it.

"Oh my God! From where we were standing I thought it was some kind of sun or star."

"It might be, but from here, it definitely looks like a tortoise."

"Cool. So, Mari said she hid it where Quetzal…whatever and the tortoise can keep an eye on it." She rolled her eyes. "I still don't understand why she couldn't just say 'I hid it here.' Must have been all the pain meds."

"Maybe. Then again, if it's in the middle of the ruins, there's not much to distinguish one pile of rubble from another." He scanned the site. "Tell you what. You go put your back to Quetzalcoatl and walk straight ahead. I'll do the same from here. Wherever we meet, that's where we'll start our search."

"Fine. Make me walk all the way over there."

"You want to stand in the yucca? Be my guest."

Jessie declined by way of raising her middle finger, then proceeded to the Quetzalcoatl pictograph. They proceeded according to Bones' plan and, after a bit of clambering over low walls and piles of lose stone, they found themselves standing before a nondescript heap of rock.

"You were right. There really wasn't a good way for her to give us the location. Assuming, of course, this is the right place." She stared doubtfully at the stones.

"We're about to find out." Bones didn't expect to encounter any snakes or scorpions up here, but he gave the pile a few kicks and a visual once-over before setting to work. In a few minutes, he'd uncovered a smooth, flat stone. He shifted it aside.

"Bingo!" Jessie exclaimed.

A gray, metal box sat in a shallow hole. Bones lifted it out and set it on the ground. "It's heavy."

"Duh. It's made of metal and is filled with paper."

"Thanks. In the future, I'll remember not to keep you in the loop."

"Did I hurt your feelings?" Jessie teased.

"Chick, you're about to make the climb down the mountain Jack-and-Jill style. Now shut up and tell me the combination."

"Mari's birth year. 1988."

Bones turned the dials on the simple lock and raised the lid. Inside lay, several manila envelopes encased in a large Ziploc bag. Bones eased the entire package out.

"Put this in your backpack," he said. "I know we probably won't run into anyone on the way back to the truck, but if we do, I don't want to be seen carrying this box." Jessie did as instructed, while Bones returned the box to its hiding place and then replaced the stones. When they were finished, he stood, brushed his hands on his jeans, and then stretched. "Dude, my back is killing me."

"If that's your way of asking for a backrub, forget it. After the Jack and Jill comment, you're on my list until you redeem yourself."

Bones was about to retort when a sound caught his ears.

"Quiet!" he whispered. He put a hand on Jessie's shoulder and the two of them ducked down behind the nearest wall.

"What is it?" she mouthed.

"Someone's coming. And whoever it is, he's trying not to be heard."

TWENTY-EIGHT

Bones and Jessie hunched down behind the wall. Bones focused, listening for the sound of approaching footsteps. Above the sound of the heavy wind that blew across the mountaintop, he could just make out the occasional scuff of sole meeting stone.

He quickly determined that only one person approached. He laid a hand on Jessie's shoulder and then dared a peek over the edge of the wall.

A stout man of late middle years stood about twenty paces away, thumbs tucked in his belt, turning in a slow circle. His facial features identified him as a member of one of the local Native American pueblos, and his weathered skin, faded jeans, cowboy boots, and oversized belt buckle suggested a rancher. He carried no weapon that Bones could see.

He relaxed. Just a local checking things out. Probably wondering to whom the pickup truck parked on the road belonged.

As the man turned away from the wall, Bones stood.

"How's it going?"

The man snapped his head around, his annoyed frown giving way to a smirk as his eyes fell on Bones.

"You caught me by surprise. For a second there I thought it was because I was getting old, but you're one of us. Sort of."

"Cherokee." Bones rounded the broken wall and approached the man, an easy smile on his face. "I'm Bonebrake, but everyone calls me Bones."

The man scowled, then reached out and took Bones' proffered hand in a powerful, heavily calloused grip.

"Nick Padilla." The man's frown returned. "I didn't know there were Cherokee in Florida."

Bones shrugged. "Originally from North Carolina. What can I say? I love the beach."

"You also love trespassing, I see."

Bones frowned. "I thought this was public land. We got our permit from the…"

Padilla waved away the explanation. "Freaking

government. This is right in the middle of Isleta land. You know why they hold on to it? Water rights, and because people like you are willing to drop twenty bucks just to see a forgery."

"Twenty-five, actually." Bones had not, in fact, secured a permit, but he had looked it up online and remembered the cost.

If it was a test, he apparently passed, because Padilla nodded. "I don't suppose they told you that a courtesy call was in order before you crossed tribal land?"

Bones shook his head. "Sorry. I didn't know."

Padilla cleared his throat, spat on the ground, and kicked sand over the fat glob of phlegm. "You know this is all a bunch of crap, don't you? The stone is a prank played by UNM students back before I was born, and the rest of this is just graffiti."

"Aren't some of the images genuine?" Jessie asked.

"A few, but nothing you can't see other places. Take him over to the Petroglyph Monument. You won't have to trespass in order to see it."

"I like unusual places," Bones said. "Just thought we'd check it out."

"If you're done, I'll walk you back to your truck." Padilla folded his arms and locked eyes with Bones. The man was determined.

Bones stared back. When pushed, his natural inclination was to push back even harder, but he didn't want a confrontation with Padilla. The man was just looking out for his people, and as a Native American, Bones had some idea of how the man felt about outsiders.

"You seem in a hurry to get us out of here," Bones said. "Is there some big secret we haven't discovered yet?"

That elicited a chuckle from Padilla. "Maybe you should be trying to discover the identity of the white dudes surveilling your truck. The blue pickup with Florida plates?"

"Seriously?" Bones kept his voice calm though his insides were ice.

"Parked behind a stand of juniper. They had just gotten out of their car and were walking toward the gate when I rolled up. They saw me and jumped back in. Whatever they're up to, I guess they don't want witnesses." Padilla hesitated. "I hope you can understand why I feel like you've brought unwanted trouble onto the pueblo."

"I stuck my nose into a situation, a guy putting his hands on his girlfriend. The dude said I could expect a visit from his friends." The lie rolled smoothly off his tongue, the shreds of truth lending it a touch of authenticity. At least, he hoped that was the case.

"It's true," Jessie said. "I know the girl."

"Seems like a strange place to do it," Padilla said, "but like I said, I guess they don't want witnesses." He looked Bones up and down. "I wouldn't be surprised if you could handle them both, but why borrow trouble?" He considered the situation for a few moments and then nodded. "Tell you what. I'll take you the back way to the ranch house. In a few hours, I'll send somebody for your truck."

"I hate to get you involved," Bones said.

"Don't mention it. Life on the ranch is boring. I almost hope they try something."

Bones laughed. "Mister Padilla, you are a man after my own heart."

The main house of Padilla's ranch was a single-story adobe structure. The central house had been added on to over the years, giving it a cobbled-together appearance. The enticing aroma of roast chile greeted them at the door, and Bones' stomach let out a low rumble.

"You got that right," Padilla said. "Mama can cook, and you're just in time for lunch."

Padilla's wife, a round woman with silver-streaked black hair and a friendly smile, greeted them warmly. Soon they were gorging themselves on homemade tortillas stuffed with a concoction of beef, green chile, and pinto beans, and washed it down with ice cold Tecate beer.

It was some of the best food Bones had ever tasted. As they drank and chatted, Padilla's tongue loosened, and he began regaling them with stories and legends he'd heard in his youth. Tales of ghosts, vanished persons and lost treasure.

"What about aliens?" Bones asked. "I know about Roswell, but are there any others?"

Padilla replied immediately. "Archuleta Mesa. That's the

place you want to check out. Well, don't actually check it out, or else you'll wind up in federal prison. At least, if the rumors are true."

"What rumors would those be?" Jessie asked.

"Supposedly, there's an underground base there—a base where the military works jointly with aliens."

Jessie cocked her head to the side. "Working jointly to do what?"

"Biological stuff. Genetic experiments on animals, maybe even humans." He took a swig of beer. "Back in the late seventies, a researcher started intercepting signals that he believed came from alien spacecraft. His search led him to Dulce, up by the Colorado border. Strange things going on up there, even today: missing or mutilated livestock, missing people, weird electro-whatever that messes with TV and cell phone reception, snatches of strange speech occasionally bleeding into radio coverage."

"Are they just rumors, or do you think there's something to it?" Jessie pressed.

"I think ninety-nine percent of UFO rumors are bigger crap than what my cattle leave behind, but there's something to this one. I've witnessed some of the phenomena firsthand when I was visiting a friend up there on the Jicarilla reservation."

"Wouldn't something like that be difficult to hide?" Bones asked.

"Not if it's under the mesa. And that's the only place it could be." Padilla sat his beer down and laced his fingers together. "Look, Dulce is a nothing town in the middle of a wide open stretch of even more nothing. That interference and those communications are coming from somewhere, and the closer you get to the mesa, the stronger they get. Compasses don't work there." His eyes took on a faraway cast, and he fell silent for a few seconds, lost in thought. Then he shook his head. "It's some X-Files stuff to be sure."

"If it's so wide open, wouldn't people see UFOs coming and going?" Bones asked.

"There are the occasional sightings, mostly strange lights, and noises, but I suspect those are terrestrial in origin. Military craft." Now Padilla leaned forward and lowered his voice. "But I think the aliens live underground."

TWENTY-NINE

"Aliens living underground?" Jessie asked, keeping her tone conversational. "I've read a little about that. Do you think there's any connection to the Puebloan legends about ant people?"

"Somebody's done her homework." Padilla grinned. "I do think there's a connection."

"Now Papi," his wife scolded, "they will think you are crazy, like that man with the funny hair on that program you watch."

"Ancient Aliens?" Bones said. "I love that show."

Senora Padilla gave a shake of her head and pushed back from the table. "I see I am outnumbered. Time to do the dishes." She stood, collected their plates, and headed to the kitchen, graciously declining Bones' and Jessie's offers to help. "You will be a greater help to me if you listen to his stories, so I don't have to." She flashed a loving smile at her husband, who grinned back at her.

"Anyway," Padilla began, "I know how this must sound, but I don't believe in most of the really out there," he bracketed the words in air quotes, "legends. No Bigfoot, Nessie, or Elvis returned from the grave."

"He faked his death," Bones said.

"Right," Padilla deadpanned. "While I don't have patience for that sort of thing, I believe there's something to these alien theories. First of all, with the sheer size of our universe, it's crazy to believe that intelligent life didn't evolve anywhere but here. To me, that's the crazy idea."

Bones nodded. The man had no idea just how right he was.

"I think extraterrestrial visitors are the source of at least some of our myths and legends, the source of some ancient knowledge, and played a part in human evolution." Padilla took a drink and let that statement sink in.

"And you think New Mexico is one of the places aliens interacted with humans?" Bones asked.

"Interacted, maybe still interact." Padilla waved his hand at the sky. "I'm not saying every UFO sighting is legit, but I believe there's something going on here. I know reliable people who have seen things. I know military guys who let a little something slip when they drank too much. There's been some crazy stuff in these parts."

"We actually did some research into an incident outside of Quemadura," Jessie said. "Have you heard of it?"

"Halcón Rock? Absolutely. That's a prime example of what I'm talking about." Neither Bones nor Jessie had to ask Padilla to elaborate. Warmed to his subject, he launched into a lengthy explanation of the underworld legends, the history of alien contact in the region, and stories of conflict.

"When I pull all the reliable bits together, it tells a story that's fairly typical of human history. We get along for a while, and then things go bad. Time passes, and it starts all over again. Archuleta Mesa is one of the better situations—humans and aliens working together. But there are plenty of times where things sour and conflict ensues. Like the battle at Halcón Rock."

"But if there are aliens living underground," Jessie said, "why doesn't anyone notice when they go to war?"

"War is probably the wrong term. More like minor conflicts, skirmishes. Maybe there aren't many of them, maybe all they really want is to be left alone. Also, there's ICE." Seeing Bones' and Jessie's twin frowns, he went on. "Initiative for Communications with Extraterrestrials."

"Haven't heard of them. Someone told us about a group called STAR."

Padilla laughed. "Bunch of rednecks in tinfoil cowboy hats. ICE is serious business."

"Government?" Bones asked.

Padilla shrugged. "Don't know. Some say it's military, others say it's para-military with its fingers in a lot of public institutions. Whichever one it is, rumors say they go to great lengths to stop anyone who gets too close to the truth. They ignore the crackpots and even a few of the people who know what they're talking about, but that's about it." He cleared his throat. "A few years ago, a friend of mine told me he'd found a way to get into the passages beneath Archuleta Mesa. Two weeks later he was found dead at the foot of a cliff, miles from the mesa. They said he fell while hiking, but I happen to know he hated hiking and feared heights. They did him in."

Bones and Jessie exchanged surreptitious glances. Was ICE the group that had been pursuing them?

"My advice to you," Padilla said, "is to stay away from Halcón Rock, or any place like it. Stick to fake Hebrew carvings and you'll be fine."

Bones laughed and raised his beer bottle. "Cheers." His phone vibrated, and he glanced at the screen. It was Amanda calling. "I need to take this."

He knew there was a problem the moment he heard Amanda's voice.

"Bones, we need you here right away. There's a problem at the hospital."

THIRTY

*"**Are you there?** I said, there's a problem at the hospital."* This time, Amanda's words hit home.

"What kind of problem?" Bones asked.

"Mari's already checked out. None of the staff would tell me anything, HIPAA rules and all that. I asked around, and the patient across the hall saw her leave with a guy."

"A guy?" Bones chewed on this new turn of events. "Did she leave voluntarily?"

"I guess so. I mean, she definitely checked out of the hospital. She wasn't hustled away or anything."

"She must have gone back to Matthew." Bones wanted to hit something. Rather, he wanted to hit one very specific someone.

"That was my thought, too," Amanda said. *"It happens in these situations. The same personality traits that get you into that kind of relationship make it almost impossible to get out."*

"I know, but still…" There wasn't much else to say.

"I'm sorry, Bones." The words hung there for a long moment. *"What do you want to do?"*

"Nothing. If she went back to him voluntarily, there's nothing I can do except hope the guy meets with an accident; preferably a grisly one."

"What do you know? We actually agree on something."

"Don't get used to it. Anyway, we found what we were looking for. I'll fill you in when we see you again.'"

He ended the call and turned back to Jessie and Padilla. Sadness painted the young woman's face. She'd obviously been listening. Padilla wore a concerned expression.

"That doesn't sound good," the rancher said.

"Some people don't want to be helped." Returning to his seat, Bones focused his attention on his beer. While Jessie and Padilla chatted about legends of underground dwellers, he sat, drinking and reflecting on his last conversation with Mari. He'd been so certain she'd turned the corner. As he ruminated, snatches of conversation drifted through.

"According to the Zoroastrians, the god Ahura Mazda

instructed his people to build underground cities to protect themselves from what he called *evil winters*…"

"He soared through the skies on a *divine chariot*. Some people think he was an alien…"

"Look at Derinyuki. Thousand-pound doors that only open from the inside…"

As Padilla shared his extensive knowledge, Bones found his interest piqued, and his thoughts drifted back to the mystery they hoped to solve. The rancher knew his stuff. Perhaps he could be of help.

"Mister Padilla, have you ever heard of the *Book of Bones*?"

Padilla jumped like he'd sat on a scorpion. He gaped for an instant and then laughed.

"So that's what's going on. All right, what's the story? You heard I keep an eye on the mountain, so you went up there hoping to meet me? You played it off as a coincidence, then worked the conversation around to the book?"

"I don't understand," Jessie said.

Padilla fixed her with a hard look and then did the same to Bones. "Lay your cards on the table or get the hell out of my house."

Bones wasn't sure what had brought about this sudden change in their host's demeanor, but he knew it would be a bad idea to hold anything back. He started with his first visit to Halcón Rock and then traced the chain of events that had brought them to Hidden Mountain. "That's the truth," he concluded. "We held back because we don't know who's after us or how dangerous they might be."

"Why don't you give up the chase, then?" Padilla asked. "Get the hell out of their way and let them do what they're going to do?"

"I'm not sure that would work. They have no way of knowing what information we might have unless they extract it from us, if you know what I mean. I've been in situations like this before, and I don't believe they'll stop until they have what they want."

"Or until someone beats them to it," Padilla said. "Is that the only reason?"

"That, and I don't run away." Bones took another swallow of beer.

Padilla nodded. "I can believe that." He cleared his throat, looked around for his wife, and then began speaking softly. "Mama doesn't like it when I mess with this stuff, but I've been interested in the *Book of Bones* for a long time. I agree with you; Gregory Glade found it and included it with his treasure. I've got some ideas about its location, but nothing solid."

"If you've got somewhere private we can talk, we'll take a look at Mari's father's work."

THIRTY-ONE

A tiny room at the corner of the house served as Padilla's office. Stacks of papers covered the simple wooden desk. A battered file cabinet, a heavy-laden bookcase, and two folding chairs completed the furnishings. Padilla cleared off his desk to make room for the documents Bones and Jessie had recovered.

Some of the work was dedicated to topics other than the Glade Treasure: cryptids, aliens, and local legends. Bones would have dearly loved to read them all, but first things first.

"Here's the info on the treasure," Jessie said. She quickly scanned each page, summarizing its contents, then passed each to Padilla.

The first page listed the clues Glade had provided. Different colors of ink indicated that the list had been added to each time the eccentric millionaire had released a new clue. The subsequent pages, which she passed over quickly, consisted of listings of possible locations, hand-drawn maps, newspaper clippings, and summaries of failed attempts to find the treasure.

"How about we flip to the end?" Bones suggested.

"Philistine," Jessie scolded. "We're almost there. I want to make sure we don't miss anything important."

"You do that. Meanwhile, I'll cut to the chase." With deft fingers, he slipped the bottom page out of Jessie's hands and laid it in the center of the desk.

"Oh, Jesus," Padilla grumbled. "It's in code."

The page was filled with lines of number pairs. Clearly, Mari's father had been confident enough in his conclusions that he sought to protect them from anyone who might get their hands on his research.

"How are we supposed to translate this?" Padilla asked.

"I've actually got some experience with this sort of thing." Bones thought back to a trip to London that eventually led him and Maddock into the Amazon. "When you see number pairs like this, it's usually referring to a line number and column number on a source document. You count down and over, and it gives you the letter."

"So, what's the document we're supposed to refer to?"

Padilla turned to Jessie. "Anything in there?"

"This is why I said we should go through the papers in order," Jessie said, riffling through the last few pages. "No documents. Just research, journal entries, and finally a photo of the Decalogue Stone." She held the image out for the two men to see.

Bones and Padilla exchanged knowing grins.

"Okay, so it's not a document," Bones said.

"You think this is the source?" Jessie asked.

"It makes a certain amount of sense. Mari did say Hidden Mountain is one of her father's favorite places."

"And when you were going through those papers," Padilla added, "did you find any mention of the stone or the mountain?"

"I didn't," she said. "So there's really no reason for the picture to be in here."

"And there's the added safeguard that the source will have to be translated from Hebrew," Bones said. "Not much of a safeguard, but it's something."

The inscription on the stone was not a perfect match for modern Hebrew, so they used a translation of the stone as a reference guide. Jessie had only transcribed a few letters before she laid her pen down.

"It's not working. We're not forming words here, just a string of letters."

Bones glanced at the transcription and grinned. "Keep going."

"But…"

"Trust me."

Jessie's eye roll was worthy of a junior high student, and not a woman in her middle twenties, but she kept going. When she finished, she slid the paper over for Bones to see.

"There you go, smart guy. Do you see a single word there? Except for this one, which might be *pygmy*, but nothing else."

"Sure do. Lots of them." Bones grinned against her withering stare.

"I got it!" Padilla pounded his fist on the desk. "There's no vowels in Hebrew. We have to figure those out ourselves."

"Exactly."

"You could have told me that from the start, and not let

me think I was wasting my time." Jessie's pout was a sight to behold, and attractive.

"But that wouldn't have been any fun for me. Usually, in situations like these, it's my friend Maddock who gets to be the smart guy. I just wanted to see what it felt like."

"And was it everything you hoped it would be?" The pout was gone, replaced by a blank stare.

"So far, so good. Now, let's figure this thing out."

"Fine." Jessie took out the list of clues and set them beside the translation. "If we assume that the translation goes in the same order as the clues, then *Through the window* becomes *lvntn.* Any ideas?"

"Lava nation," Bones said.

"Lav.. la ventana?" Padilla asked.

"The answer to *Through the window* is the Spanish word for *window*?" Jessie tapped the end of the pen against her chin. "I'll write it down for now."

They spent the next thirty minutes working at the translations. Some sets of letters, such as *ccv*, defied their best efforts, but others came quickly. *Where God looks down* translated to *big skylight*, and *Where small secrets are hidden* became *pygmy forest*.

"Okay," Jessie said, "for *Where the moon stands in line* we've got *chnfcrtr*s. Thoughts?"

"Chain of craters," Padilla said immediately. "And *Esau and Jacob*, that's *Twin Craters*." He pointed to another line. "And now that I think about it, *ccv* is *ice cave*." He folded his arms, rocked back in his chair, and smiled.

"You seem pretty sure," Jessie said.

The old rancher nodded. "I am. Because I know exactly where it's hidden."

THIRTY-TWO

"This is like walking on hot asphalt." Jessie mopped her sodden brow and looked out over the lava fields of El Malpais National Monument. Located one hundred miles west of Albuquerque, the forbidding yet beautiful landscape included lava flows, sandstone bluffs, cinder cones, craters, and caves. And heat. Lots of it.

"So what, exactly, does El Malpais mean?" Bones asked.

"The Badlands," Padilla said. The old rancher had insisted on joining them on their search, much to his wife's chagrin. Despite her protests, he'd helped Bones recover his pickup, and the three of them had set off along Interstate 25 and into the parched lands that lay between Albuquerque and Flagstaff, Arizona.

"That's a good name for it." Bones sidestepped a spiny cactus that had somehow taken root in a fissure in the hard, black surface. "I wonder what the natives made of this place?"

"Most considered it a place of evil for obvious reasons. Mostly they kept to the sand bluffs and came no closer. It's not like there's game or water out here on the lava flow."

"Yeah, you'd have to be an idiot to cross this thing." Bones grinned at his two companions. Padilla chuckled, but Jessie ignored him. Bones worried that the heat was getting to the young woman and she was too stubborn to tell him if she was overheating. She dismissed his concerns with curt reminders that she was the native New Mexican, and not he.

"Not many people come here, that's for sure. Tourists and hikers mostly. Every once in a while, someone dumps a body out here, but that's about it. Used to be treasure hunters out here. Until the murders, that is."

Bones frowned at Padilla. "Wait a minute. Were they looking for Glade's treasure? And what murders?"

Padilla chuckled. "This was a long time ago. There are all kinds of legends of treasure hidden out here: bandits hiding stolen loot, miners holing up in a cave or lava tube and dying, even Spaniards searching for gold came here. At least, that's what the stories say."

"What about the murders?" Jessie's eyes darted to and fro as if danger lurked somewhere on the obsidian landscape.

"A local fellow, nicknamed Old Man Gray, used to patrol the area, trying to chase off treasure hunters. He was quite a character—rode with Teddy Roosevelt and the Roughriders, came back and worked as a lawman for a while. Anyway, he hated the treasure hunters. Said they trespassed on his land and even dug up a family grave once. Locals knew to steer clear of him, and outsiders figured it out pretty quick. Except for two fellows who must have seen a withered old man, he was near a hundred years old at the time and thought they had nothing to worry about. Old Man Gray killed them, but he died before he could stand trial."

"So he won't be shooting us today," Jessie said. "That's a relief."

"Mister Padilla," Bones said, "when this is over, I want to spend a few days drinking beer and listening to your stories."

Padilla threw back his head and laughed. "You're the only one, son. The only one."

Bones stole a glance over his shoulder but saw only scorched blackness. They'd left La Ventana, the prominent sandstone arch, far in the distance. Padilla had recognized its name, as well as those of several other nearby landmarks, as belonging to this area. Their final destination lay somewhere up ahead.

"I hope it's cooler in the cave than it is out here," Jessie said.

"Believe me, once we get down in there, you'll freeze your backside off," Padilla said. "Being out here in this heat is only going to make it seem even colder in there. We should take our time making our way down."

"Don't you think it's kind of weird that Gregory Glade hid his treasure in a place that's so popular with treasure hunters?" Jessie asked.

Padilla made a noncommittal gesture. "I don't know. Not many folks took the treasure stories seriously. The Old Man Gray incident sealed it. What better place to hide a treasure than a place that's been combed over for a century and nothing found?"

"What if someone's already combed over the cave?"

Jessie's normal, upbeat personality seemed to be wilting in the intense heat.

"The treasure hasn't been found," Bones said.

"Not many people know about this cave," Padilla added. "It's only accessed through a narrow cleft in the rock, followed by a tight squeeze through a lava tube. The rangers don't list it on any park maps because they don't want the bats disturbed. They've had problems with White-Nose Syndrome, and…"

"Hold on. Bats?" Jessie stopped in her tracks and gaped at Padilla. "Down in the cave where we're going?"

"Yes, a whole colony of them. We'll have to disinfect all our gear before we go inside. Bones being from back East, there's a chance he could be carrying the fungus on his boots."

"Am I on a different planet than the two of you? Why would we go into a cave filled with bats?"

"Bats are cool," Bones said. "They're basically just flying mice. Sort of."

Jessie's jaw dropped even further. "I… forget it. Let's just go. But if those things suck my blood, I'm coming back to haunt both of you."

Bones decided not to correct Jessie's misconceptions about the tiny mammals, at least not just yet. Perhaps fretting over vampire bats would distract her from the heat.

"You forgot the bright spot," he said. "If we're going into the bat cave, there's a chance we'll run into Catwoman."

Jessie turned and walked away, an upraised middle finger her only reply.

THIRTY-THREE

The cool air hit Bones like a wave as soon as they descended into the cave. The rocks beneath his feet were smooth and slick and shifted under his weight. He warned the others to proceed with caution as they worked their way deeper into the darkness.

"I don't see any bats." A faint note of hopefulness rang in Jessie's voice.

"They'll be a lot deeper in," Padilla said. "But they're not going to mess with you. I promise.

Jessie pursed her lips. "Yes, but do *they* promise?"

They continued to move forward and downward. Their headlamps sliced narrow blades of light through the curtain of darkness. Being closed to the public, this cave had no well-worn path to follow. Instead, they made their own way, investigating side passages, many of which were blocked by rock falls, clambering over loose rock piles, and sliding down steep inclines.

Bones soon grew impatient. He liked to move fast, and this slow going did not suit him at all.

"We'd better find something soon," he muttered.

"What's that?" Jessie asked.

"Nothing. Just ready to get out of here and have a beer. Or three."

"Come on. Can you honestly tell me you aren't having fun?" Thrilled by the prospect of discovery, Padilla was like a kid on Christmas Eve. The old rancher couldn't keep the bounce from his step or the exhilaration from his voice.

"For me, this falls into the 'been there, done that' category," Bones said.

"Well, don't spoil it for the rest of us," Jessie reproved.

"Look out! Bats!" Bones shouted.

Jessie shrieked. Her hands clamped down on his arm, and she looked around wildly, the beam of her lamp zig-zagging over the ceiling of the cave.

"Where?" she gasped.

Bones chuckled. "Just messing with you."

"You ass!" Jessie punched him on the arm.

"Hey! Don't spoil my fun," Bones teased.

"You are pushing it, Bonebrake." The young woman lapsed into resentful silence as they continued onward.

"How long have we been at this?" Padilla asked when they eventually stopped for a rest.

Bones checked his watch. "Almost two hours."

"Maybe the treasure is not here," Jessie said glumly.

Bones placed his hand on her shoulder and gave it a squeeze. "Don't give up just yet. Looks like there's still a lot more cave to explore."

"I thought you wanted to get out of here."

"I'll finish the job first. I always do."

They hadn't gone more than two hundred feet when Padilla, who had taken the lead, let out a shout of surprise. He fell, accompanied by the clatter of tumbling rocks. His headlamp bobbed up and down, mostly down, as he fell. Bones made a grab for him, but he was far too late. The older man came to a stop at the bottom of a sharp incline, a good twenty feet below.

"The floor gave way underneath me," Padilla groaned. "I know. Nothing like stating the obvious."

"Are you all right?" Bones asked, relieved to hear the old man's voice.

"I hurt my ankle, but I think my pride is what's really injured."

"Don't even worry about it," Bones said. "You're hardly the first to take a fall."

Carefully, he and Jessie picked their way down the steep, rocky incline, to where the rancher sat checking his ankle.

"It's not too bad," Padilla said. "I can keep going."

"You should stay here and take a rest," Jessie said. "Bones and I will go on."

Padilla shook his head. "Not a chance. I came this far, and I'm going to see it through." Gritting his teeth, he heaved himself back up onto his feet.

"Really, Mr. Padilla, you should stay here." Jessie turned to Bones. "Tell him."

Bones looked at Padilla. The rancher narrowed his eyes and slowly shook his head.

"He's not going to give in on this," Bones said. "No sense

in wasting our time arguing."

"But if he gets hurt…"

"If he gets hurt, we'll leave his stubborn old ass here for the vampire bats."

Jessie's eyes flashed toward the ceiling and then back to Bones. "You are such a jerk."

Bones winked. "Yeah, but you love me anyway."

"If I roll my eyes at you any more than I already have I'm afraid I'll go cross-eyed."

"Nobody appreciates my humor," Bones said

Jessie put her hands on her hips. "Humor? Is that what you call it?"

"You are not a nice girl."

"Ouch. That one hurt." She mimed stabbing herself in the heart.

"I hate to be the grumpy old man here, but how about we get on with it? Unless you two want to get a room and leave me to do this myself." Limping, Padilla lumbered ahead.

Bones turn to Jessie. "What do you say? Want to get a room?"

For a moment, Jessie stared daggers at him. Then, with a shake of her head, she turned and stalked away after Padilla, muttering something that sounded like "asshat" under her breath. Laughing, Bones followed along behind.

An hour later, Jessie had had enough. She halted in her tracks, folded her arms, and looked up at the ceiling. "How much longer are we going to do this? There's nothing here but passages and more passages. Well, now just a single passage, and it looks like we won't be going much farther."

She was right. Up ahead, the way, which had grown progressively tighter, narrowed to a near-impassible width.

"We go much farther, we'll need a child to squeeze through some of these passages," Padilla said.

"Or a trim, athletic gymnast." Bones raised his eyebrows at Jessie.

It took the young woman a moment to get his meaning.

"Oh, hell no!" She took a step back. "You're not sending me ahead by myself. The bats are in there somewhere."

"Relax," Bones said. "I'm only talking a little farther. Slip through there, and see if the way opens up. If it keeps getting narrower, we'll go back."

"And what if I get stuck?"

"If it makes you feel any better, I'll tie a rope around your waist so I can drag you back."

Jessie made a face. "No thanks. If I'm trapped down here forever, you'll have to settle for me haunting you for the rest of your natural life."

"Deal."

Jessie turned, took a few deep breaths, steeling herself, and then shot one last glance at Bones. "You suck, you know that?"

Bones gave a single nod. "It's been said."

Without another word, Jessie moved deeper into the passageway. Bones and Padilla watched until the glow from her headlamp vanished.

They waited.

"You think she's okay?" Padilla asked after a few long, silent minutes.

"She hasn't called for help. That's a good sign."

"Yeah, I just worry about what might happen. A drop-off, a collapse, falling stalactites." He glanced up at the stone spikes that hung above their heads.

"Well aren't you a ray of sunshine?"

Just then, Jessie's voice pierced the quiet.

"Bones! Get in here right now!"

THIRTY-FOUR

Bones pressed forward, Padilla close behind him. The way grew narrower, and he felt his chest constrict under the pressure of squeezing his bulk between the tightly-spaced walls. The cold of the rock surface seemed to seep into his body as he inched forward.

"Are we going to be able to get through?" he called to Jessie.

"I think so."

"That's comforting."

"It will be tight in the middle, but it opens back up pretty quickly after that."

"I think there's a *that's what she said* joke in there somewhere," Bones called back.

Over the sound of Padilla chuckling, he heard Jessie swear.

"Just get your butts in here."

Bones sucked in his gut and, with supreme effort, forced himself into the narrowest part of the passageway. A slight flash of anxiety, the overwhelming feeling of suffocating, and then he was through. He turned, took Padilla's hand, and hauled the bulky rancher through behind him.

Just as Jessie had said, the passage opened up, and they found themselves in a large chamber. Stalactites dangled high above their head, peeking out from the midst of a mass of dark, furry creatures. Bats.

"Man, it stinks down here," Padilla said.

"Guano. Lots of it." Bones crinkled his nose and looked around at the bat droppings that coated virtually every inch of the cave. "This is what you were in such a hurry for us to see?" he asked Jessie. "A carpet of bat crap?"

"First of all, way to go me for not freaking out when I saw all these bats." Jessie pointed at the ceiling. "But no, that's not what I wanted you to see." She cast a meaningful glance down toward her feet.

It took Bones a moment to realize what he was looking at. A grinning, human skull peeked out from beneath a pile of bat droppings. He trailed the beam of his headlamp across the floor and saw bits of a rib cage sticking up and, nearby, a skeletal hand clutching a pitted sword.

"Who was this guy?" Padilla asked, moving closer to the skeletal remains. He kicked at what looked like a guano-covered rock. The object tipped over, revealing a concave underside. "It's an old helmet. Spanish, maybe?"

Bones nodded. "The shape is right, and that would be the most logical guess for this part of the country. And check out his leg. That's a bad break." He pointed to the remains of a shattered tibia sticking up above the crust of dried excrement.

"I wonder if he was alone, or if his buddies left him behind?" Padilla mused.

"Look, if you are trying to guilt trip me into hauling you out of here on my back, give it up. You can limp your way out of here."

Padilla let out a hearty laugh. "Boy, I like you. A man after my own heart."

Bones looked to Jessie. "So you found an old dead dude. Anything else?"

Jessie let out a deep, tired sigh. "Oh my God. Open your eyes." She turned and directed the beam of her headlamp toward the far wall, where stalagmites and stalactites framed an arched entrance into another cavern.

Bones grinned. "Let's check it out."

He led the way into the adjacent cave, and what he saw there brought a smile to his face. Despite the refuse left by the colony of bats, he could make out three rows of broken down benches. Beyond them stood a simple stone altar, and carved into the far wall was a large cross. Covered in filth, bats dangling from the crossbar, the symbol of Christianity carried a sense of foreboding about it.

"The legends are true!" Padilla said. "The Spaniards really did build a church down here."

"It doesn't make sense," Jessie said. "I mean, why put a church deep inside a cave in the middle of a lava field that, frankly, looks like the pathway to hell?"

"Because it's not that kind of church." Bones had realized what was so wrong about this place. "Take another look at that cross."

The others followed his line of sight and the beam of his

headlamp back to the cross on the wall. This time, they too saw it immediately

"It's upside down!" Jessie said.

"They were Satan worshipers?" Padilla asked.

Bones shrugged. "Something of an occult nature was going on down here. No wonder they hid so far away from prying eyes."

"This is all so wrong. It's like something out of a horror movie," Jessie said

"Or an adventure movie," Padilla said. "I wonder where Glade hid the treasure."

"My money is on the altar," Jessie said.

"I don't know," Bones kidded. "Kind of obvious, don't you think?"

She turned and flashed Bones a sly smile. "Tell you what, if I'm wrong, we'll get that room together. Deal?"

Bones suddenly felt guilty for having flirted with the young woman. He liked her, which was why he knew he should keep his distance. A nice girl like her deserved a better guy than him. He forced a smile. "An old guy like me? I'm sure I'd only disappoint you." He tried to play it off as a joke, but a curtain of crimson drew across Jessie's face, and she turned and hurried toward the altar.

"She's a smart, pretty girl. A good girl," Padilla whispered. "What's the problem?"

"That's exactly the problem," Bones replied. "She's a good girl, but I'm not a good guy."

Smiling, Padilla clapped Bones on the back. "You just proved that you *are* a good guy. Trust me on this." The old man followed Jessie toward the altar, leaving Bones with his thoughts.

Jessie squatted down behind the altar and frowned. "I don't see anything. It's just a solid block. Where do you think it could be?" Bones noticed that she didn't quite meet his eye as she spoke.

He looked all around, scanning the floor and the walls of the chamber for any indication of where the treasure might be hidden. And he was certain the treasure was here. This was an ideal place for someone like Gregory Glade to hide it. But where could it be?

As his beam swept across the back wall, the light fell upon an unnaturally even patch. He drew his knife and moved closer until he stood directly beneath the inverted cross. He scraped the surface with the edge of his blade. The crusty layer of bat droppings fell away, revealing a smooth patch of stone about the size of a breadbox.

"Looks like you've found something." Padilla moved to Bones' side. "Yes, I think you're onto something." He ran his calloused hand across the surface and looked it up and down. "It's rough, like adobe."

"Stand back." Bones reversed his knife and slammed the hilt into the center of the patch. It shattered under the force of his blow. He quickly cleared away a large opening and Jessie, her upset seemingly forgotten, shouldered past him and peered into the dark space. "There's a chest in there!"

Bones reached inside and took out a brass bound wooden chest. "This thing's heavy."

"That's a good sign," Padilla said.

"Set it over here." Jessie pointed to the altar.

Bones placed the treasure chest atop the stone block and stepped back. The three of them stood there in silence, relishing the moment of discovery.

"I can't believe it," Padilla said. "All my life I fancied myself a treasure hunter, but this is the first time I've actually found anything. Thanks for including me."

Jessie reached out and gave the old rancher's hand a squeeze. "We couldn't have found it without you."

"So," Bones began, "who wants to do the honors?" He turned and looked at Jessie, who stuck out her lower lip.

"Is that how you're going to try to get back into my good graces?"

"Look, chick if you don't want to open it, I will." Bones took a step toward the chest, but Jessie reached out and grabbed him by the arm.

"Okay fine I'll do it." She took a long look at the chest. "There doesn't seem to be any lock. I wonder why?"

"No need," Padilla said. "Glade is giving the treasure away, so why lock it up?"

Jessie nodded. "Makes sense." She stared at the chest for another long moment, and then reached out and grabbed the lid. She pulled, but it didn't budge. She took a breath and pulled again. Still nothing. "It's stuck." She mumbled.

"What was that?" Bones asked.

"You heard me."

"Are you saying you want help? Because you seemed pretty sure that you wanted to do it by yourself."

"Just get over here and help me," Jessie snapped.

"All right. All right. Never say I don't follow orders." Bones wedged his knife under the edge of the trunk lid and worked at it until it broke free. Then he stepped back and once again Jessie tried it. This time, it opened.

"Oh my God." Jessie's amazement was understandable. The chest brimmed with gold. Bones saw Spanish doubloons, small gold bars, and modern coins, including Krugerrands and pesos. Jewels glinted red, blue, and green under the triple lights of their headlamps.

"I can't imagine how much this is worth!" Jessie said.

"I know somebody who won't be taking out any student loans next year." Padilla laughed.

Jessie frowned, and then the blood drained from her face. "What do you mean?"

"Finders keepers," Bones said. "The three of us found it together so…"

Jessie wobbled and would have fallen had he not grabbed hold of her. "Easy there. Do you need to sit down?"

"In the middle of all that crap? No thanks. I'm just…"

"In shock?" Padilla offered. "I just hope my old lady doesn't have a heart attack when I tell her."

"I imagine the various artifacts will have to be returned to wherever they came from," Bones said, holding up an Egyptian scarab. "And speaking of artifacts, let's not forget what we came here for." He opened his backpack and began transferring items from the chest into the pack. Jessie and Padilla did the same with their own packs. It didn't take long to empty the small chest, and when they reached the bottom, Jessie let out a cry of delight.

"That's it! It's got to be!"

Bones picked up a leather bound object roughly the size of a paperback book. Slowly, he drew back the cover, exposing the contents.

"The *Book of Bones*."

THIRTY-FIVE

Although night had fallen, the black rocks of the lava field radiated heat. Still, it was a jovial group that made their way back to Bones' truck. He didn't know if it was the joy of a job well done or the thrill of newfound wealth that excited his companions. Probably a bit of both.

"How are you going to spend your share?" Jessie asked

"Don't jinx us," he replied. "I've found and lost enough treasure to last a lifetime."

"You are such a pessimist," she said. "What could possibly happen between here and the truck?"

"Funny you should ask. Everyone get down." Bones dropped to a knee in the shadow of a rock pile. Jessie and Padilla hunkered down beside him.

"What is it?" Padilla whispered.

"I saw someone moving on the horizon. Just a shadow flitting past the moon."

"Maybe it's not someone who means us any trouble," Jessie said. "Could be another tourist."

"Doing some sightseeing on a black lava field in the dark?" Bones said. "I don't think so. Besides, I could tell by the way he moved that he was trying to be stealthy. He just didn't do a good job of it."

"How do you want to play this?" Padilla asked.

Bones knew they didn't have much time. He quickly considered the situation. "All right, here's what we're going to do."

As he outlined his plan, he quickly rearranged the treasure. They had brought the empty treasure chest along, and he now filled the bottom with a layer of loose stones, added in the gold bars, a few gold coins and jewels, and all of the various artifacts. He put the rest of the treasure in a backpack, hid it in a crevasse and covered it with rocks. Then he handed Jessie a map of the park and tucked the *Book of Bones* into her backpack.

"Keep moving north and stay out of sight," he instructed. "Try not to use your flashlight or your phone if you can help it. It will make you easier to spot in the dark. If you think someone is after you, hide. If you're not at the meeting spot when we get there, I will come and find you. I promise."

The young woman didn't ask how he could make such a promise. She merely nodded, took a few steps away, and then froze. She whirled around, gave him a quick kiss on the lips, and then vanished into the darkness.

"I still think you need to reconsider about her," Padilla said, staring in the direction in which Jessie had gone.

"I'll think about that later." Bones drew his Glock and handed it to Padilla. "Right now, we've got a trap to set."

Bones moved slowly, careful not to let the treasure and loose rocks inside the chest rattle around. He estimated he was a half a mile from where he had parked his truck. A half-mile of open ground that offered no cover. He had no doubt the truck was being watched. The question was, where exactly were the men who were following them? He took a deep breath and headed for the parking lot.

He hadn't gone more than a dozen steps when a voice called out.

"Stop right there."

Bones kept walking.

Bang!

A shot rang out, sparks flying where the bullet grazed the lava field only a few feet in front of Bones. This time, he stopped.

Maybe I do have a death wish. Better not tell Maddock.

"Put the chest on the ground and take twenty steps back," the voice instructed.

"Then I do the hokey pokey, and I turn myself around?" Bones asked.

"My orders did not specify whether or not I should let you live, so keep trying to piss me off. It will make my decision that much easier."

"Fair enough." Slowly, Bones placed the chest on the ground, raised his hands above his head, and moved away.

"Hands behind your head. Down on your knees."

This time, Bones followed orders. Soft footsteps, sounding like thunder in the quiet night, echoed across the lava field. A muscular man of medium height, carrying a 9 mm, appeared out of the darkness. His facial features were Korean, but his accent was one hundred percent Boston.

"Flat on the ground," he snapped. "I don't trust you."

"Bro, you're the only one here with a gun. You'll get no trouble out of me."

"Somehow, I doubt that." The man turned his head toward the lava field. "Mixon! Cooley! I got him. Come on back."

A minute later, his companions appeared. Cooley, a bear of a man, towered over the stocky Mixon. The taller man carried a Glock, similar to the one Bones favored, while the shorter man wore a revolver holstered on each hip, gunslinger style.

"Not bad, Scott," Cooley said. "Maybe we'll keep you around after all."

"You wish," Scott said. "I'm just biding my time with you jokers. And I think this is my ticket to a promotion." He tucked his pistol into the waistband of his pants, reached down, and hefted the treasure chest. "Damn! This thing is heavy. What's in here?"

Bones held his breath. He would be fine if the men would simply take the treasure chest and be on their way, but if they looked inside it…

"It doesn't matter what's inside," Mixon snapped. "That's above your pay grade. Our job is to get this to the boss."

"What do we do with this guy?" Cooley inclined his head toward Bones.

Mixon shrugged. "It's your call. You're the one who loves killing people."

Cooley shook his head. "I don't love it. It's part of my job. And since genius over here said our names…" He shot a meaningful glance at Scott, who shrugged. "Better safe than sorry." He raised his Glock.

The night erupted in thunderous gunfire as Padilla, hiding nearby, opened fire. Cooley's body jerked as slugs tore into him, and he fell in a heap. Mixon spun toward the direction from which the shots had come and opened up with both barrels, but Padilla was no longer there. An instant later, a single shot rang out, the bullet taking Mixon in the forehead.

At the sound of the first shot, Scott had made a run for

the parking lot, pistol in his right hand, treasure chest tucked under his left arm.

Bones watched him go. No point chasing him down. The guy was an idiot, but he was still armed, and dumb luck was a distinct possibility. And, unless he missed his guess, the man's boss would neither see Scott nor the treasure chest. Besides, what mattered most was Bones, Padilla, and Jessie were safe. And, almost as important, they had what they had come for.

THIRTY-SIX

Mari strained against the bonds that held her wrists fast. The sharp edge of the plastic zip tie cut into her soft flesh. She grimaced and twisted, but only succeeded in wrenching her shoulder, sending a jolt of pain stabbing through her and eliciting a grunt. Her ankles, similarly trussed, scarcely budged as she struggled to free herself.

She blinked the sweat out of her eyes and cast a baleful glance at the air conditioning unit as it rumbled and clattered in futile resistance against the southern New Mexico heat.

"If you are going to kidnap me, you could at least put me up in a decent hotel," she grumbled to the empty room.

Kidnapped. She chewed on the word, trying to make herself believe it. She'd been through a lot in her life, but being abducted was something that happened to people in bad Lifetime movies, or those close to Liam Neeson; not to her.

"I really need to improve my taste in guys."

As if on cue, the doorknob rattled, and after a few failed attempts, the person on the other side managed to unlock it. Matthew stepped through the doorway, his face a cloud of fury at even this minor inconvenience. Mari would have laughed at him were the situation not so dire.

"You need to let me go," she said for what must have been the thousandth time.

Matthew shook his head. Somehow the mute response was worse than a flat out refusal.

"You don't even need me anymore," she said. "You obviously know where you're going."

After he'd taken her from the hospital at the point of a gun concealed in his jacket, they had driven back to Quemadura, Mari tied up in the backseat, sweating even more profusely than she did now. Matthew had gone into his father's house and returned a short while later grinning broadly. From there, they'd made the long drive down to Carlsbad Caverns, the jackass boasting all the while about how he had cleverly hacked his father's computer and learned where Sheriff Jameson and his cronies were headed. Mari had summoned enough courage to point out that logging on to someone's home computer and opening their email wasn't exactly hacking. That had taken the wind out of Matthew's sails, but only for a few minutes.

Summoned the courage. That was a laugh. *Why did I let him take me so easily? There were people all around at the hospital. I should have argued with him or called for help. He wouldn't have shot me.*

She wasn't certain that last bit was true, and that was what had compelled her to *come quietly*, as the saying went. Still, it grated at her. Why couldn't she be brave? What inside of her was so broken that she allowed this pitiful excuse for a man to enter and reenter her life, and control her so completely?

She thought about Bones, the stranger who had seemingly set all of this in motion. She had liked him, and thought he might have liked her a little bit. That was a real man. He walked with a quiet confidence that said he had nothing to prove to anyone. He had none of Matthew's bluster, no false bravado. He was perfectly comfortable in his own skin. And that was why Mari hadn't given him a chance. She had never been comfortable in her own skin, and Bones scared her.

Matthew sat down on the bed next to her, the box springs squeaking under his weight. He reached out and put a tentative hand on her shoulder. She tried to twist away, sending another jolt of agony through her shoulder.

"You loved me once," he said quietly.

She managed a mute reply of her own—a sour frown and a single shake of the head.

Matthew chuckled. "Yes, you did. We both know it." His hand left her shoulder and moved to the top of her head. "You will love me again." He stroked her sodden hair. "I promise."

"Just kill me," she said. It was not bravery; merely words born of hopelessness, but she meant them.

Matthew's hand froze. Slowly he closed his fingers into a fist, grabbing a handful of her hair in the process. He jerked her head around, forcing her to face him.

"I'm not going to kill you. At least not yet." He paused to let that sink in. "Even if you never care for me again, you're still of use to me."

Mari's confusion must have shown in her eyes because he answered her unspoken question.

"You're a bargaining chip. That big Indian has a thing for you. If I have to, I'll trade you for what I want."

That big Indian has a thing for you. Mari hated the way her heart skipped a beat at those words. Here she was in the worst, most precarious position she'd ever been in in her life, and she was indulging a schoolgirl crush.

"So it's true," Matthew whispered. *Damn. Maybe he really could read her like a book.* Matthew stood and cracked his knuckles.

Mari thought he might hit her and was surprised to realize she didn't care. She supposed she was past caring about anything where Matthew was concerned. As she expected, he cocked his fist, but then he froze.

"You *will* love me." He turned and walked out the door leaving Mari alone with her self-loathing.

THIRTY-SEVEN

The path into Carlsbad Caverns seemed to go on forever. It wound down at a steep incline through majestic chambers that looked like something out of a fairy tale, albeit a dark and foreboding one. Only Padilla, who had visited here many times before, seemed immune to its magnificence. Even Bones, who had seen more than his share of amazing things, found himself slack-jawed at the sight. Perhaps he would return someday and give this place the time and attention it deserved.

Jessie glanced up at him, reading his thoughts. "When this is over, you should bring me back here. I think I deserve it after all I've been through."

Bone smiled and winked. He wasn't ready to think about that right now. They moved on in silence until, after a descent of what felt like hours, they found themselves in the midst of a horde of tourists.

"Where did all these people come from?" Jessie asked. "We nearly had the place to ourselves on the way down."

"Most people take the elevator from the visitor center," Amanda said.

"Lazy bastards." Padilla grinned. "If an old man like me can make the hike, they can too."

"I don't know. The walk was tough enough. I don't relish the idea of doing it again, except uphill this time." Krueger looked back in the direction from which they had come, a slight frown creasing his brow.

"I'm glad you said it and not me." Padilla knuckled the small of his back. "My brain says I can handle it no problem, but my body is raising some objections."

"The place we're looking for is not too far from here." Bones unfolded a map of the caverns, and they all gathered around. He tapped their destination on the map.

"I remember this place," Padilla said. "I wanted to take the guided tour, but Mama was having none of it."

"Let's split up. As a group, we make a motley crew. Might draw attention" Bones felt Jessie's hand close on his.

"You three go ahead. We'll follow along behind you," the young woman said.

They navigated the crowds of tourists, trying their best to blend in. It wasn't difficult, considering how focused the visitors were on their surroundings. Everywhere Bones looked he saw something wondrous. It was hard to believe that it lay beneath such dry, barren land up above.

Despite their fascinating surroundings, Bones kept an eye out for anything amiss. It wasn't long before he grew suspicious of two men who seemed to be following along behind them. Each wore cargo shorts and a T-shirt, and carried maps of the caverns. At first glance, they blended with the rest of the tourists, but he sensed something was wrong. For one, they made too much of a show of checking their maps. The caverns were large, but the concrete paths lined with metal rails weren't exactly difficult to follow. And every time he glanced in their direction, they quickly took an interest in a stalactite or other formation. They were faking it.

Finally, Padilla halted in the middle of the pathway. He turned, swept the caverns with his eyes, and then leaned back against the railing. Krueger and Amanda did the same. Bones kept walking toward them.

"What are you doing?" Jessie whispered. "I thought we were pretending to be in separate groups."

"I think we've been made. Don't look around."

Jessie grimaced. "I wasn't going to."

"Yes, you were."

"All right. I was, but you don't have to be smug about it."

"Smugness is one of my many charms." He halted about five paces from the others, turned and rested his hands on the rail. "I think we're being followed," he said, not looking at them.

"What do we do?" Padilla asked, still staring off into the distance.

"You guys keep wandering around. Jessie, you stay close to them. I'll see if I can get them to follow me."

Padilla checked his watch. "Hurry. The tour group should be coming up at any minute."

"Got it." As the others wandered away, Bones took out his map and gave it a long look. Next, he took a quick look around, not too subtle, but not too obvious. At least he hoped. He tucked the map into his pocket, turned, and strode away. He didn't exactly walk fast, but neither did he stroll. He walked with a sense of purpose, his eyes fixed on a spot in the distance.

The two men didn't look at him as he passed by. Bones kept moving. As he turned a corner, he dared a quick glance back. They were following him. Good. Well, it wasn't *good* that whoever was after them had caught up yet again, but at least he knew who they were and where they were. Now to deal with them.

No sign marked the entrance to the King's Palace. That seemed to be the way here. Bones supposed that drawing attention to the out-of-the-way spots would only encourage tourists to wander off to places they weren't supposed to be and get themselves lost. That was fine by him. It meant fewer witnesses.

He heard voices in the distance and waited. A few minutes later, a family wandered past. The father, busy trying to keep the children corralled, didn't notice the smile his wife flashed at Bones. He merely nodded in return. He didn't do married chicks; not literally, not figuratively. When he was alone again, he vaulted the rail and hurried down the steep, winding pathway, as it doubled back again and again. He didn't turn on his flashlight. His pursuers would figure out where he went soon enough, if not immediately, but he didn't want to draw the attention of any other tourists that might pass this way.

It wasn't long before the flashlight became a necessity. Bones had excellent night vision, but this was something else entirely—an utter absence of light that one could find only when caving, or at the lowest depths of the sea.

He clicked on his Maglite. The red filter he had placed over the lens cast a dim light a few feet in front of him. It was enough to see by, but not enough for someone to spot him unless they were close. He assumed there was a tour group somewhere up ahead, and he had no desire to draw their notice.

He made his way deeper into the caverns along a well-worn path. He passed through more magnificent chambers that already seemed a bit mundane after all the wonders he had seen thus far. He swept his beam back and forth, looking for the perfect spot. He didn't want to kill these men if he didn't have to. He supposed he could simply hide and let them pass him by, but that would only gain him and his friends a short lead, and that would be virtually worthless if their pursuers had figured out exactly where Bones and the group were headed next.

He finally came to a place where a curtain of stalactites cascaded down from the ceiling to meet a wall of stalagmites. Behind them lay an open space more than large enough for a man to hide. *Perfect.* He hefted a stone the size of his fist and hunkered down in the darkness.

Minutes later, he heard the soft shuffle of people trying to move quietly and almost succeeding. He tensed, ready to spring. A dim glow announced the men's entrance into the cavern. They played their flashlights around, searching. A narrow sliver of light swept a few inches above Bones' head, but he was well hidden. After a few more moments looking around, the men moved forward. The path carried them within a few feet of where Bones crouched. When the men had passed him by, he made his move.

Unlike his pursuers, Bones actually could move in silence and his long legs allowed him to move at a cautious pace and still close the distance in an instant. He didn't need his flashlight—the men were silhouetted in the glow of their own lights, and it was child's play to make his attack.

The man on the left was bigger, more muscled, and strode forward confidently, while the fellow on the right continually looked around, his nerves on edge. Bones judged him the less dangerous of the two, so he went after the bigger man first.

Clutching his rock in both hands, Bones clubbed the man across the back of the head. His knees turned to rubber, and he collapsed in a heap. His partner could only manage a "What...?" before Bones cracked him across the forehead.

With both men down, Bones bound them with their own shoelaces, stuffed their socks in their mouths, and gagged them with strips torn from their shirts. He then dragged them into the same place he had hidden only moments before. When this was over, he would call in an anonymous tip to make sure the two men were found. But for now, they'd remain here, where they couldn't interfere.

He took a deep breath. Time to find out if he and the others were right.

THIRTY-EIGHT

The others were still waiting when Bones returned. He gave a small nod and a thumbs-up in answer to their unasked questions and smiles spread across their faces.

"Jessie and I will go on down," Bones said. He would've liked to take Padilla with him as well, but the rancher was needed to look out for the others in his absence. Besides, Jessie was the most athletic of the group, and would be better able to navigate her way through the caverns below. After a quick look around to make sure no one was watching, the two of them vaulted the rail and began their descent.

The path immediately fell into a smooth, steep decline, but there was no time to set a rope. They skidded down to the bottom, then regained their feet and moved on. After only a few steps inky blackness enveloped them, and they paused to strap on their headlamps before continuing.

They worked their way down to a series of ladders. Bones went first. The metal rungs were cold in his hands and slick with condensation, but they were sturdy. He descended quickly, with Jessie right behind him. As expected, she had no problem making the climb down. She moved so nimbly that Bones wondered if he should caution her against overconfidence, but decided against it. *The girl's doing fine.*

By the time his feet touched solid ground he found himself on high alert. A noise had caught his attention—a scuffing of boots on stone. Someone was coming.

Jessie hadn't heard. "What's wrong?" she whispered

One finger held to his lips was his only reply. They moved to the nearest wall and pressed themselves into the deepest shadows. Soon, the beam of a headlamp appeared far above them, and then another and another. Bones relaxed when he recognized the person in the lead.

"Padilla," he said

"What are they doing?" Jessie asked.

"I can tell you what they're not doing: following orders."

He waited, foot tapping impatiently, as the others hurried

down the ladders.

"Don't bother," Amanda said before Bones could chastise them. "You didn't actually think we would be left behind, did you?"

Bones grimaced. "I suppose not. Let's get on with it."

Matthew moved quickly through the meandering clusters of gawking tourists. He gritted his teeth, exhaled impatiently. His first inclination was to force his way through. After all, he had something important to do. They didn't. But, he knew it wouldn't do to draw unnecessary attention to himself. The Indian and his friends were somewhere up ahead. He'd seen the man's truck in the parking lot. Matthew needed to find them, and be discreet about it.

It didn't take him long to realize he would need help if he was to find his quarry before they got away. He looked around and spotted a man in a National Parks Services uniform.

"Excuse me," he began. "I'm looking for a friend of mine and I wondered if you might have seen him."

The man smiled. "I see thousands of people every day, so unless your friend really stands out in a crowd…"

"Oh he does, believe me. He's about six-and-a-half feet tall." Matthew held a hand slightly above his own head to indicate his quarry's height. It galled him. He hated being shorter than anyone. "Indian fellow. Can't miss him," he added.

The man furrowed his brown, and he scratched his chin. "An Indian that big? Are you putting me on?"

Matthew forced a laugh. "He's a big fellow, no doubt." Matthew was finding it harder and harder to keep his grin in place.

"What kind of Indian?"

Matthew hesitated for a moment then understood the man's question. "Oh! Our kind of Indian. Not the other kind. You know," he pressed a finger to his forehand, "A feather, not a dot."

That was the wrong thing to say. The man's expression soured like milk left out in the sun. "Haven't seen him," he snapped.

"Hey I didn't mean anything by that," Matthew said, but the man was already walking away. "Dammit."

"You're looking for the big Indian guy?" a voice behind him asked. He turned to see two attractive young women smiling at him. Their black hair, almond eyes, and cocoa butter skin marked them as some kind of Chinese; Korean maybe. Matthew flashed an easy smile. He'd always wanted to hook up with a Chinese girl. Maybe this was his chance.

"Yeah, I am."

"He's a friend of yours?" one of them asked. Matthew looked her up and down before replying. She had a trim, athletic figure and straight white teeth. Her friend was equally cute. In fact, if it weren't for the speaker's ponytail, he wouldn't be able to tell them apart. Were they twins, or was that just the Chinese thing? He wasn't sure. "Yeah, he's a friend of mine. Have you seen him?"

"Oh, we definitely saw him." The girls giggled.

"He kind of stands out in a crowd, you know?" The second girl said.

"He's pretty tall, isn't he?" Matthew kept his grin locked in place.

"Yeah," Ponytail said. "That too."

"What do you mean?"

"Are you kidding? He's so hot."

"Scorching," her friend added.

Matthew felt his grin freeze into a grimace. "Do you know where he went? We got separated."

The girls nodded like twin bobbleheads. Ponytail pointed toward a nondescript stretch of railing. "He was standing there, and then when I looked again he was gone." She made a pouting face that sent a shiver down Matthew's spine. Man, she was cute.

"Don't be sad," he said. "Tell you what, give me your number and he and I will take you out for dinner later. How's that sound?"

The girls exchanged glances.

"Come on. Dinner's on me. Do you know of any good Chinese places around here?"

The twin tightening of the girls' mouths told him he'd said the wrong thing again.

"We're Korean," Ponytail said.

"I know! I mean, that's what I thought... I mean that's

what I said."

She folded her arms. "Let me give you a tip. There's nothing funny about casual racism."

"I'm not racist. My girlfriend's Mexican." He didn't need their exasperated sighs to know where he had stepped in it that time. The girls turned in lockstep, hooked their arms, and strode away.

Matthew only spared them a wistful glance before putting them out of his mind. He had gotten what he wanted. He knew where the Indian had gone.

THIRTY-NINE

Padilla took the lead while Bones brought up the rear. They moved swiftly, the marvels of this, the Lower Cave, flashing by too quickly for them to admire. Padilla, who seemed to know everything about Carlsbad, pointed out some of the sites. In the Rookery, marble shaped formations called cave pearls covered many of the surfaces and seemed to glow with an ethereal light under the beams of their headlamps. Among the many stalactites and stalagmites were hollow tubes called soda straws.

"Tourists used to snap these off and take them as souvenirs," Padilla grumbled. "Morons."

They squeezed through narrow passages barely wide enough for Bones to fit through, crawled through low tunnels, and slid down steep inclines. Finally, they came to a halt. Bones felt rather than saw a large open space in front of them.

"This is the largest chamber of the lower cave," Padilla said. "We're going to have to be careful on this next stretch."

"Why?" Jessie asked. "We are far below ground in total darkness."

"True, but right up there," Padilla pointed to a spot hundreds of feet above them, "is a place where people can look down into this cave from up in the main chamber."

All eyes moved to the opening far above, where a faint yellow light shone. As they watched, a pair of tourists, at least Bones assumed they were tourists, moved to the rail and looked down into the chamber. They stayed for only a moment, unable to see anything in the darkness below, and moved on.

"What do we do?" Amanda asked. "We can't cover that much space in the dark. We'd get lost."

"We'll use one light," Bones said. "I'll go first. We'll make a chain. If anyone sees someone up above, just say 'freeze.' We'll all stop, and I'll turn out the light until they're gone."

"Sounds like a game you play at a slumber party," Jessie said.

"You got a better idea?"

"Touchy, touchy. I wasn't criticizing, just saying."

"Fine. Let's get a move on." Instead of turning on his headlamp, Bones took out his Maglite with the red filter. It would not afford nearly as much light, but neither was it likely to be seen from a distance. "Everybody stay together and take small steps. I'll warn you of any obstructions."

Feeling like a mother goose trying to herd her goslings across a street, he led the group out into the cavern.

They moved slowly and steadily, periodically halting when they saw movement above. It was an odd feeling, standing frozen in place in the pitch black. Bones found his already-sharp sense of hearing heightened. At least, it seemed that way. He heard the out-of-shape Krueger panting, Padilla's stomach rumbling, and Amanda muttering about how much time they were losing. Jessie remained silent, standing close to him and squeezing his hand tightly in hers. She was so close he even caught a whiff of her shampoo — coconut. Perhaps his sense of smell had grown stronger in the darkness too.

Along the way, they examined formations that were noted in the *Book of Bones*. These, of course, did not bear the modern names, but those assigned to them by Native Americans so long ago. The spot where twin stalactites and stalactites met, known today as *Colonel Bowles* formation, was called the *Fangs of the Viper*. The large, rounded formation was the *Great Turtle*. They went on like that, slowly finding landmarks, and picking their way across the cold, slick rock. Finally, they came to a halt on the far side of the chamber, where a mass of bat skeletons were embedded in the stone.

"If these are the *stone bats*," Amanda began, "the last clue is the *mouth of the demon*."

"I think we're going to have to turn on our headlamps and hope we aren't spotted," Krueger said.

"Let me." Bones took another look up at the opening to the main cave, scarcely visible at this angle. He thought someone up above would be hard-pressed to see them unless they were hanging out of the opening. Nonetheless, he would only take a quick look. He switched on his headlamp and looked up.

"That's it!" Padilla pounded him on the back.

Directly above the mound of bat skeletons, a curtain of

stalactites hung across a low, wide opening. Still higher on the wall, a bulbous outcropping formed the nose, and two shallow caves, perfectly spaced, the eyes.

"Do you think there's anything back there?" Jessie asked.

"Only one way to find out." Bones laced his fingers together, and Jessie stepped into his hand. He lifted her with ease, and she hoisted herself up and over the ledge and squeezed her lithe form into the largest of the openings.

"What do you see?" Bones asked.

"Come on up," her voice answered. "You've got to see this."

FORTY

Matthew froze and switched off his headlamp. There was that sound again. A dull scrape like someone or something moving through the passageway behind him. Bonebrake and his group were somewhere up ahead, but what could be following him? The lower cave tour only ran once a day, so there should be no one coming in behind him. Probably it was his imagination. Echoes of his own footsteps, maybe. Still, he quickened his pace.

He stumbled along, occasionally barking his shin and just barely managing to suppress a curse as pain shot up his leg. He was tempted to turn back. This place was colder than a hooker's heart. The dampness soaked into him, and the oppressive feel of stone all around him set his nerves on edge.

More than once he told himself Bonebrake was on the wrong track. Carlsbad was such a popular tourist destination, he reasoned, that anything of interest down here would have already been found. But that wasn't true. Certain sections were still being explored, and many were off-limits to the public. A man could spend a lifetime exploring the caverns and never learn all its secrets. It was the thought of Bonebrake uncovering one of those secrets, a secret Matthew had worked so hard to unlock, that kept him going.

A large cavern loomed up ahead, and he quickly covered his headlamp, allowing only enough glow for him to see a few steps ahead. He paused at the mouth of the passageway and peered in. He saw little in the blackness, save for a dim light on the far side of the cavern. As he watched, a large figure silhouetted in dull, red light, clambered a few feet up the cave wall and then disappeared from sight.

Bonebrake! He must have found a passageway of some sort.

Matthew smiled. He was on the right track after all.

"Is that your son up there?" Gilmour whispered. "I don't want him getting in the way."

"He won't." Jameson tried to hide the frustration that

welled up inside him. He was fed up with Matthew. The boy's antics had caused nothing but problems for the sheriff. As a youth, he'd been the town bully, and kept it up into young adulthood. That alone had kept Jameson scrambling to keep his job and deal with the aftermath of Matthew's shenanigans. And now he was a grown-ass man, and he'd turned into the sort of person Jameson despised—an abuser and a cripplingly insecure narcissist. To top it all off, he'd run afoul of ICE, and put Jameson at risk too.

Hell, the boy wasn't even his, though Matthew didn't know it. He was the product of his mother's affair, back when Jameson was drinking too much and paying too little attention to his home life. He'd raised Matthew as his own, done his best, and he'd failed.

"I'm sorry, Luce," he whispered to the soul of his deceased wife, just in case there really was a heaven, and she'd made it in.

Gilmour stared at Jameson. The beam of his headlamp made it impossible to read the expression on the ICE agent's face, but Jameson thought he knew what the man was thinking. Jameson had failed to keep Matthew in check, and he was now a liability.

"What do you think happened to your two?" Jameson asked, deflecting the focus away from his own failings. The two ICE agents Gilmour had sent ahead of them had neither been seen nor heard from.

"They're morons." Gilmour pressed his lips together in a tight frown. That was, apparently, the end of that.

They watched as Matthew stole across the cavern, stopped on the other side for a moment, and began to climb. A few moments later, the darkness swallowed him whole.

"Looks like there's a passageway over there," Gilmour said. "Let's go."

Jameson swallowed the bile rising in his throat. He dreaded what was about to happen, but it was the way it had to be.

FORTY-ONE

Jessie led them on hands and knees through a veritable forest of stalagmites, their condensation-slicked surfaces dancing under the beams of their headlamps. A carpet of cave pearls set up a luminescent glow beneath them. It was like an alien world. Bones hoped that was a good omen.

Finally, the passageway came to an end.

"This can't be it," Amanda said. "I'm battered, soaked, and filthy. If it's all been for nothing…"

"It hasn't been." Jessie turned and looked back at them. "Everyone scoot back a little. I need some room." The young woman nimbly shifted to a seated position and, bracing herself against a rock formation, raised her feet and drove them into the wall in front of her.

The surface of the wall cracked. A few more kicks and she'd opened a hole just large enough for them to crawl through. She lay flat on her stomach and wriggled through. An instant later they heard her call out to them.

"You can stand up in here. Come on through!"

When they were all on the other side, they paused for a moment to enjoy the feeling of standing on their feet again.

"I don't mind telling you that just about did me in," Padilla said.

"It was like the world's longest planking session," Amanda agreed, wincing and rubbing her abdomen.

"So," Bones said, turning to Jessie, "how did you know the passageway was here?"

"I knew it had to be somewhere. I mean, all the clues up to this point had been reliable. I noticed that the other side of the wall was covered with guano. When I took a closer look, I realized that the base of the wall wasn't stone, but dried guano that had built up over the years."

"That's a bunch of crap." Bones winked at her.

"That would explain why no one has found this passageway," Krueger offered. "Explorers assumed they'd reached the end of the line."

"And, unlike me, they wouldn't go smashing through

walls," Jessie said.

"Don't worry about it. You did good." Bones gave her shoulder a squeeze and led the way down the passage.

They wound down a long, sloping tunnel. Here, the floor was smooth, and no rock formations hindered them. It was almost as if someone had carved the by hand. Bones knew that wasn't the case. He saw no chisel marks or other signs of the stones being worked, but the change was noticeable, nonetheless.

The passageway finally leveled off. They rounded a turn and stopped short. Before them stood a simple, arched entryway. And beyond it…

Jessie gasped. "Aliens!"

The room put Bones to mind of a hogan—the traditional Navajo home. It was a circular, domed room. A sipapu, the symbolic indentation found at the center of a kiva, was carved in the bedrock at the room's center. Petroglyphs—familiar images of the so-called "Ant People" covered the walls. But it was none of those features that captivated Bones.

Four alcoves, evenly spaced around the room, were carved into the stone walls. Inside each, upon a stone bier, lay the remains of a bizarre-looking being. Moldering scraps of fabric clung to skeletal remains. Beads once stitched to burial garments lay scattered atop the biers. Each clutched a weapon—a bow, knife, or spear.

Bones moved to inspect the nearest figure. It, like the others, was no more than five feet tall, with fine bone structure. His gaze climbed to the face and locked there in disbelief.

"Holy crap." The structure was very much that of the stereotypical alien. An oversized cranium gave way to a narrow face. Large, round eye sockets and a tiny mouth completed the bizarre scene. What set this skull apart from other supposed aliens were the four bony appendages extending from the top of the head.

"Ant People," Krueger breathed. "They were real. They even had antennae." He reached a trembling hand toward the remains.

"Don't." Bone's seized his wrist an instant before he could touch one of the appendages.

"Sorry. Got carried away." Krueger took a step back and gazed at the remains with wonder and longing.

The others gathered around, talking excitedly. Amanda took out her camera and began snapping pictures. Jessie did the same with her smartphone, while Padilla, grinning, bemoaned the limits of his primitive flip phone.

While they chatted, Bones circled the room, taking a closer look at each skeleton. Three were so-called "Ant People", but the fourth was different. She, for the bone structure clearly marked her as female, had a human face. Unlike the others, she was garbed in an odd mesh, like the strands of a spider's web. And instead of four snakelike appendages, eight spidery legs framed her skull.

A spider woman.

A sinking feeling suddenly lay heavy in Bones' gut. He made another circuit of the room, giving each skeleton a closer inspection. He drew his knife, placed the tip under the chin of one of the Ant Men, and cautiously lifted it a few centimeters. Just enough to confirm his suspicion.

"Dammit all to hell." He sheathed his knife and let out a long, slow breath of disappointment.

No one heard his muttered curse. Jessie, beaming, seized his arm and pressed her body against his.

"What do you think this means? Were the Ant People really aliens or were they the source of the alien stories?"

Bones looked down at her smiling face, reluctant to deliver the news. He was spared the task when a loud voice boomed over the din of conversation.

"Everybody freeze or this girl dies!"

FORTY-TWO

Bones turned to see Matthew standing just inside the doorway. He held Amanda in a chokehold, a revolver pressed to her temple. Even in the uneven light cast by a myriad of headlamps Bones could see determination in the man's eyes, and a touch of madness.

"If you do anything to her, you die," Bones said. "You know that, don't you?"

"Wrong. First I turn her brain to oatmeal and then I back down the tunnel and wait for you to come at me. Lots of choke points for me to choose from. Do you like your odds?"

"I've taken out better than you." That was true, but Bones knew his words rang hollow. He wasn't going to let Amanda die, much less anyone else from his group, if he could help it.

"Maybe," Matthew said. "But there's also Mari to consider."

Bones didn't think his stomach could churn any more than it already had, but Matthew's words put him at the edge of throwing up. "What are you talking about? Where is she?"

Matthew chuckled. "She's somewhere safe, but if I don't come back for her she'll die... slowly. People need food and water, you know? I've even got the pics to prove it."

For an instant, Bones considered drawing his pistol, gunslinger-style, and taking a shot at Matthew, but he dismissed that thought immediately. Even if he was fast enough, only a small fraction of Matthew's head was exposed. He'd never make that shot. Hell, Maddock probably couldn't make it, and Maddock was better with a handgun than anyone Bones had ever met... not that Bones would ever admit it, of course.

"So, what's it going to... don't do it, old man!" Matthew took a half-step back, dragging Amanda with him, his eyes moving back-and-forth between Bones and Padilla, who had nearly succumbed to the same Old West instinct that had almost overcome Bones. "Everybody on the ground face-down or people start dying."

Bones couldn't believe this turn of events. The elation of a few minutes before had dissolved in the bitter libation of defeat.

"Do what he says," he told the others.

Matthew didn't lower his guard for an instant. Once everyone lay side-by-side in the center of the room, he instructed Bones and Padilla to slide their weapons over to him, including Bones' Recon knife and Padilla's hunting knife. Only then did he shove Amanda roughly to the ground. Now, with a pistol in each hand and a third tucked into his belt, he loomed over them, the corners of his mouth tilted upward in a manic grin.

"I want the book," he said to Bones.

"I didn't bring it along," Bones said.

"Who should I shoot first? Your choice." Matthew leveled his pistol at Jessie. "I could shoot her in the liver and let you listen to her scream. It wouldn't bother me, but I imagine a woman in pain brings out the white knight in you."

"It's in my pack," Krueger blurted. "I'll give it to you. Just don't shoot." Carefully, the man removed his drawstring backpack and tossed it to Matthew.

To Bones' chagrin, Matthew kept his eyes on his captives and his weapon steady, even as he bent to pick up the ancient book.

"You lose," Matthew said.

"Not really," Bones said. "It's useless."

"What are you talking about?" Suspicion flared in Matthew's eyes.

"These aren't aliens. They're ordinary people with Ant People burial masks."

"You're lying."

Bones shook his head. "This is just some sort of shrine to the Ant People. It's culturally significant, probably interesting to archaeologists. But there are no aliens here."

Matthew aimed both barrels at Bones. His knuckles turned white with the pressure he put on the grips, and his arms trembled slightly. "Stop lying."

"Check for yourself. The masks look realistic, but they're just masks."

Keeping one pistol trained on Bones, Matthew sidled over to the closest bier. He looked the skeleton up and down, then holstered the pistol in his right hand, reached out, and lifted the burial mask.

"No," he whispered.

"Told you." Despite his disappointment at not finding aliens, Bones derived a measure of satisfaction at Matthew's own frustration. The man moved to another body, removed the mask, and shouted a curse.

"This must be your first treasure hunt," Bones said. "I could have told you, I've chased a lot of rainbows in my life, and there's almost never a pot of gold at the end."

Matthew now quaked with rage. He rushed to the third Ant Person and raised the mask. He let out a scream of pure rage, whirled, and flung the mask across the room.

That was when Bones made his move. He sprang to his feet, snatched the spear from the grip of the closest skeleton, and hurled it at Matthew, who realized an instant too late what was happening. The spear sliced across his forearm just as he squeezed the trigger of his pistol.

The boom reverberated through the chamber and Bones felt the bullet take a chunk out of his shoulder as he plowed into Matthew. They hit the floor with Bones on top. Holding Matthew's gun hand in place, he rained punches down as Matthew twisted and struggled to buck the big man off of him. Hot rage boiled inside Bones and, for a moment, he considered choking the life out of their would-be captor, but something stayed his hand.

"Where's Mari?" he demanded.

Matthew, his face slick with blood, snarled and spat at Bones. Bones raised his fist to deliver a blow, but he froze as a new voice rang out.

"That's quite enough. Get off of him and I won't shoot any of you."

FORTY-THREE

Sheriff Jameson and another man, whom Bones didn't recognize, stood just inside the chamber. Each held an automatic pistol—one trained on Bones, the other on Padilla, who was just reaching to pick up the revolver that had fallen from Matthew's grasp.

"Step back and sit down," Jameson said.

Bones and Padilla complied immediately. When they'd moved to the center of the room and dropped to the floor, Matthew lurched to his feet, collected his pistol, and turned burning eyes on Bones.

"You've made your last mistake," he said.

Bones ignored him, instead directing his attention to Jameson and the other newcomer.

"I know you," he said to Jameson. "And I assume your friend here is from ICE."

The man nodded but didn't reply.

"Gilmour is ICE?" Matthew addressed the question to his father, who didn't reply.

"And those idiots who tried to follow us," Bones continued. "Are they yours, too?"

The corners of Gilmour's mouth twitched. "I don't claim them as mine, but they're part of our organization. Are they dead?"

"Not worth killing. Let us go and I'll tell you where you can find them."

Gilmour laughed. "Not a chance. In fact, I almost wish you had killed them. They're a pain in my ass."

A brief silence fell, which Amanda finally broke. "If you're looking for aliens, you're wasting your time. There's nothing here but some Indians with Ant People masks."

"You've got it wrong. ICE doesn't want to *find* aliens. At least, not in the way you probably think. We protect humankind from them."

"Doesn't ICE stand for Initiative for Communications with Extraterrestrials?" Krueger asked.

"Not quite. It's the 'Initiative for *Control of*

Extraterrestrials.'

"But Dulce…" Padilla began.

Gilmour raised his hand. "Dulce was a failed attempt to work with the aliens instead of against them. We'd been fighting these things, mostly underground, for decades. We learned to communicate with them, even managed to make some progress on the scientific front, but it eventually went south."

"Let me guess," Bones said, "you wanted to chop them up and see what's inside, and they didn't like that."

"We're well past the slicing and dicing stage of research. Now we're doing DNA analysis and the like. Problem was, the bottom-dwellers, as we call them, found out about it. They didn't mind, but they decided they'd give a few of our guys the same treatment. They didn't wait for us to obtain cadavers. It went downhill from there. Now we're all about neutralizing threats, sealing off entrances to their world."

"Why don't they just blast their way out?" Krueger asked, his curiosity clearly overwhelming the perils of the situation.

"They could, I suppose, but they have to know it would get ugly if they did. They've been doing the live and let live thing for a while now, so we're sealing up entrances and erasing evidence. The last thing we need is for nosy conspiracy theorists," the man quirked an eyebrow at Krueger, "to find their way to the below world and cause an incident."

"Did you build the door at Halcón Rock?" Krueger asked.

Gilmour shook his head. "From the looks of it, that thing had been there for centuries, maybe more. In any case, no one will find it again. There was a major collapse of the passageways leading down to it."

Matthew rounded on his father, fists clenched. "Dad!" The word came out like a schoolboy refusing to eat his broccoli.

"Shut up, boy," Jameson said. "It's over and done with. You could have caused an incident, you know?"

"I'm still going to write my book," Matthew mumbled. "I've worked too hard just to let it drop. Besides, most people won't believe me, but a few will."

"We'll discuss that after we've taken care of business. We need to blow this place, just to be safe." Jameson took Matthew by the arm and steered him toward the passageway leading out.

"We'd better do the Indian first," Gilmour said. "He looks like he just might try something."

Bones tensed to spring at the man. He probably had no chance to save himself or the others, but he would try.

"No!" Matthew shouted.

Bones couldn't believe it. Matthew was taking their side? That thought was dashed with Matthew's next words.

"I want him to suffer. Let them stay down here until they suffocate, or starve to death, whichever comes first."

"That's cold," Gilmour said, "but it's fine by me." He raised his voice. "We're going to back out now. Anybody tries anything, he gets gut shot, and I promise you I don't miss."

"Just let us go," Jessie pleaded. "We didn't find anything down here."

"But he told us about ICE," Bones said. "Once he did that, he couldn't let us live."

"Smarter than you look." Gilmour flashed a wry smile, and he and Jameson backed out of the cavern, weapons at the ready, leaving Bones and the others alone to their fate.

When the men had disappeared into the darkness, Padilla turned to Bones. "Tell me you've got a plan."

Bones nodded. "Absolutely I do."

FORTY-FOUR

"Can I trust you to stand guard?" Jameson said to Matthew as they rounded a sharp bend in the passageway. "Gilmour and I need to set the explosive charges and we don't need interference from the Indian."

Matthew glared back at him, blood oozing from his nose and a cut on his forehead, painting his battered face scarlet. "Not a problem." He turned, a pistol in each hand, and fixed his eyes in the direction of the tunnel. He stood, feet wide apart, guns pointed forward like a video game character.

Jameson shook his head, wondering again how he'd failed so badly as a parent. Matthew's posturing at least made what Jameson had to do a little more palatable.

He pushed those thoughts from his mind as they chose the perfect spots to set the plastic explosives Gilmour had brought along for just this purpose.

When the detonators were placed, and all was ready, Gilmour gave him a long look. "It's time. Do you need me to do it?"

"He's my screw-up. I'll take care of it."

His stomach doing somersaults, Jameson strode back to where Matthew stood guard. He'd tucked his pistols into his belt and now stood, elbows akimbo, like a gunslinger ready to draw. Jameson vowed to slap him if he dared declare himself anyone's "huckleberry".

Matthew glanced over his shoulder. "No sign of them. Bunch of cowards."

"You're armed; they're not. They wouldn't stand a chance coming down this narrow tunnel." Privately, Jameson wondered if Bonebrake could, in fact, find a way. The man was highly competent and supremely self-assured. It was a touch surprising he hadn't made a bid for freedom. No matter now. It was almost over.

"Damn right they wouldn't stand a chance," Matthew said. "That Indian jumped me from behind. He could never take me one-on-one." He didn't meet Jameson's eye as he made his declaration.

"Hopefully, we won't have to find out." Jameson hesitated for a split-second, but Matthew didn't notice. *It's the right thing to do.* Slowly, so as not to draw Matthew's notice, he drew his pistol and raised it like a club. *At least he won't know what's about to happen.*

He gritted his teeth and struck. Matthew went down in a heap.

"I'm sorry, boy. You brought it on yourself." Holstering his pistol, Jameson turned, rounded the corner, and made his way back to Gilmour.

The ICE agent was waiting, arms folded, an expectant look on his face.

"It's done," Jameson said. "Let's blow this place and get out of here."

"So, what's this brilliant plan of yours?" Amanda didn't look at Bones. Instead, she glowered at the passageway where Matthew, his father, and Gilmour disappeared. Tension trembled through her body. She looked ready to chase after the man who'd held her captive minutes before.

"We were so excited to find this chamber that we forgot one more clue."

The others frowned, but Jessie's face brightened almost immediately.

"The spider's web."

"Most of these bodies represent Ant People, but not this one." Bones indicated the body with eight legs protruding from the head. "This is Grandmother Spider."

Only Krueger appeared to know what he was talking about. The man smiled and nodded eagerly.

"Depending on the mythology, Grandmother Spider, Spider Grandmother, or Spider Woman, either serves the gods or is a deity herself. To some, she's the Earth Mother. To others, she's an intercessory between humankind and the creator."

Padilla pounded his fist into his palm. "I remember now! According to the Hopi, she opened the path into the fourth world—our world."

"She caused a hollow reed to grow to the sky, and it emerged as a sipapu in the fourth world," Krueger added. "The people climbed through it into our world."

"You think this Grandmother Spider," Jessie eyed the body with a glint of reluctance in her eyes, "guards a sipapu that leads down into the third world?"

"Maybe not the third world as the Hopi described it, but it makes sense she'd guard the way to a *world below*, don't you think?"

"Only one way to find out," said Padilla.

They examined the body carefully, looking under it for anything that might resemble a sipapu, the symbolic hole found at the center of a kiva, but found nothing.

"Maybe underneath the slab?" Padilla suggested.

Unlike the other three biers, a stone slab lay upon this one, supporting the body that represented Mother Spider. Working together, the five of them heaved and hauled until it finally shifted a few inches. A few more minutes' work and they managed to pivot the top end two meters—far enough to reveal a gaping hole leading down into the earth.

"You did it!" Jessie marveled. "I can't…"

A thunderous boom rolled over her words, and the floor shook beneath their feet.

Bones cast his eyes up toward the ceiling, fearing it might collapse, but he saw no cracks in the solid surface. "They blew the tunnel," he said.

"Should we check it out?" Padilla asked.

"Might as well. If there's any chance of getting out the way we came in, that would be preferable to climbing down to who-knows-where."

"And what if we can't get out?" Amanda asked.

"Then we pay a visit to the world below."

FORTY-FIVE

Bones could tell in a glance that there would be no returning to the surface through the lower cave. Jameson and Gilmour had done a thorough job of bringing down the tunnel. Huge chunks of solid rock lay piled from floor to ceiling. So much for that idea. But now they had another concern.

"He left his own son down here to die?" Padilla asked. Around a sharp bend in the cave, shielded from the blast, Matthew lay semi-conscious, bleeding from a cut in the back of his head.

He opened one eye at the sound of Padilla's voice.

"You have got to be kidding me." His words came out slurred, his gaze wet. "You are the last people I want to see right now." He made a weak grab for his pistol, which lay a few feet away, but Bones stamped on his wrist.

"Yeah, that's not happening. You want to live, you keep still." He and Padilla retrieved the pistols and knives Matthew had taken from them, along with Matthew's own pistol. He also retrieved The *Book of Bones*, which Matthew had tucked into his belt.

"Just kill me already, you dirty redskin piece of…" His words died in a squelched grunt as Bones drove a foot into his gut.

"Manners. After all, we're not the ones who tried to kill you."

Confusion slid across Matthew's glassy eyes. "Nobody tried to kill me. The charges went off too soon." He paused, swallowed hard. "I don't think my dad made it."

"Don't bother explaining it," Bones said to Padilla. "He'll figure it out soon enough." He turned back to Matthew. "Tell me where Mari is."

"Go to hell."

"Wrong answer." Lightning fast, Bones snatched Matthew's wrist and bent his hand backward.

"Go ahead. Break it," Matthew grunted.

"That's not the plan." Bones drew his knife and pressed the tip beneath the nail of Matthew's index finger. "I'll ask again. Where's Mari?"

Beads of sweat formed on Matthew's forehead, but he kept his silence as Bones pushed down on the knife.

"Okay! Okay! I'll tell you!" Details spilled out: the name and location of the motel where she was being held captive, and the room number.

"You're lying." Bones twisted the knife, and Matthew screamed.

"I told you the truth!"

"Tell me again, and if I don't believe you, I'll cut the finger off."

Matthew began to blather, adding a few details but keeping his story consistent.

When Bones was satisfied the man was telling the truth, he wiped the blade of his knife on Matthew's pants, stood, and turned to Padilla.

"Let's get out of here."

"You don't think we should, you know, finish him?"

"Be my guest." Bones could tell by the look in Padilla's eye the man wouldn't murder Matthew, good idea or not. "I don't think he's going to be a problem, but just to be safe." He drew back his foot and kicked Matthew in the head, just hard enough to turn the man's lights out. "That'll keep him. Now, let's see what's down below."

FORTY-SIX

The tiny passageway beneath Spider Grandmother's head was sharply angled—not quite a vertical drop, but hardly an easy descent. Bones led the way, taking full advantage of the hand and footholds carved into the stone. The surface was cool and slick; several times he lost his grip and skidded a few feet before arresting his fall.

Padilla came next, the logic being that, if he fell, he wouldn't take out the rest of the crew like so many bowling pins. Jessie, aside from Bones the most athletic, followed, then Amanda and Krueger. The bookish man at least had a bit of experience with this sort of thing, having once joined Bones and Maddock on a brief foray into Egypt.

After a laborious climb down, they finally reached level ground. The passageway, straight and narrow, led to a familiar sight; familiar, at least to Bones.

"It's another door, like the one at Halcón Rock."

A gleaming, silver door barred their way. Like the one he'd seen previously, it bore no markings and had no visible, hinges, locks, or knobs. This door, however, had something the other did not—a square pad set in the wall to the left.

"It's beautiful," Krueger breathed. "Flawless." He took a step back and grinned. "Who wants to be the one to touch the pad?"

"You can do the honors if you like," Bones said. Privately, he wondered if the door would open for them.

Krueger stepped forward and pressed his palm to the pad. Nothing happened.

"Damn," Padilla cursed.

Krueger pressed harder, the veins in his forearms bulging with the effort. The pad began to glow. A wide, thin beam of green light shone forth and ran up and down Krueger's body. Then the light spread to take them all in.

"I don't like this," Amanda said as the light enveloped her.

After several seconds, it stopped. And then, with barely a whisper, the door slid to the side.

"Holy crap," Bones said. "It actually opened."

"You first, big guy. This is your rodeo."

He felt Amanda's hands on the small of his back, nudging him forward, but he was already moving. Wondering what lay on the other side, he stepped through the doorway.

He'd expected to find something remarkable on the other side, but there was nothing to see save a continuation of the passageway. He continued on, the others falling into step behind him.

"I wonder why it opened for us," Padilla said. "If it was meant to keep people out…"

"We don't know what it was meant for," Bones said. "Gilmour said the trouble between humans and these aliens, or Ant People, or whatever they are, is fairly recent, but this entrance hasn't been used since the Puebloans created that shrine.

"Centuries upon centuries ago," Krueger said. "Maybe millennia."

"That's what I'm thinking. Hopefully, whoever is down here had a good relationship with the natives."

"Good thing we've got the native leading the way," Amanda said.

Bones rounded a corner, and his sarcastic reply died on his lips. He froze.

"What is it?" Jessie whispered.

"Everybody stand right where you are," he said, "and slowly put your hands above your heads."

FORTY-SEVEN

Matthew came to with a pounding headache. The Indian had kicked him in the head, he remembered that much, but that wasn't all, was it? No, he'd first been knocked out by flying debris from the explosion. But… no, the timing was all wrong. His dad had been talking to him, then the next thing he knew, he was looking up at the Indian and the old rancher.

Bile rising in his throat, he understood. The Indian hadn't lied—Sheriff Jameson, his own father, had left him here to die. The man had chosen ICE over his own son.

"Son of a…" Just then he became aware of another pain, burning and stabbing, at the tip of his finger. In the beam of his headlamp, which miraculously still burned, he saw sticky blood covering his hand, and the memory of the Indian sliding his knife beneath Matthew's fingernail swam to the surface. His stomach lurched and a wave of dizziness passed over him. How could so small a hurt cause him so much pain?

"I'm going to find that redskin, and I'm going to kill him."

"…put your hands above your heads." Bones followed his own instructions, spreading his fingers wide to show he wasn't holding anything, and raising his hands above his head. Hopefully, this was sufficient to convey he meant no harm because the last thing he wanted to do was threaten the being that stood before him.

The creature stood about five feet tall. Its large head, bulbous eyes, and thin, sinewy arms and legs very much resembling the so-called "Alien Greys" or "Roswell Greys" of UFO folklore. Its chest and hips were thickly muscled, and its waist narrow, giving its torso a segmented appearance, like that of an ant. Adding to its antlike appearance were a second set of arms, stunted with claws where the hands should be, extending from its abdomen, and a pair of silvery antennae, so fine as to be almost invisible in the near-darkness. These were in constant motion. Given that the creature had no visible nose or ears, Bones assumed the antennae did the work.

The Ant Person, as Bones found himself thinking of the

being, was clearly old. A hint of yellow tinged its gray skin, which hung in folds at its joints. Cradle moons of purple hung beneath its eyes, and specks of white hair dotted its chest.

I hope old Ant Men aren't as crotchety as their human counterparts.

The being clutched a silver rod tipped with a gleaming purple crystal. Bones had seen a few artifacts very much like it in his time, and they were not to be trifled with.

"Is that an Atlantean weapon?"

At the sound of Krueger's voice, the Ant Man let out a hiss, baring thin, spiky teeth, and leveled his weapon.

"It's similar," Bones said. "Let's not find out, though."

"Did you say *Atlantean*?" Amanda piped up.

"Not now," Bones said.

Its large eyes were glossy black, but somehow Bones knew it was staring at him. He stared back, uncertain how to proceed. As he searched for the words, it held out one hand, palm up, and tilted its head forward a fraction.

Bones almost laughed at how human the gesture was. Apparently, "What the hell do you want?" was universal. Literally.

"We want to get out." He pointed up at the ceiling. "Out," he repeated.

The Ant Man seemed to understand. It moved to the side and pointed down the tunnel.

"We communicated with it!" Krueger said.

Once again, the being hissed.

"I don't think he likes white people," Bones said. "And you're the only one in the group who fits that description, so maybe you should hang back a little."

"Agreed." Krueger sounded disappointed.

Bones once again took the lead, and the Ant Person fell in step behind them. After ten minutes, a greenish glow appeared in the distance, soon growing bright enough that they could turn off their headlamps.

They emerged on a narrow ledge. Down below, a magnificent sight greeted them.

They were looking into a broad cavern, illuminated by the glow of green crystals set in the ceiling. The walls were honeycombed with stairs and cliff dwellings, all sliced out of the rock with laser precision. At the cavern's center was carved a sunken, perfectly round, room. A stone bench encircled the space. To one side, walled off by three vertical stones, a small carcass, perhaps a rat, roasted on a spit over glowing embers. A well lay at the center, the surface of the water shining in the emerald glow.

A group of Ant People, fewer than a dozen, went about their daily activities. Some tended children, while another sliced up chunks of a mushroom-like fungus. None paid any mind to the intruders into their realm.

"It's like a Sci-Fi Mesa Verde," Krueger whispered. "The Anasazi dwellings must have been modeled after this."

"And that spot in the middle is the inspiration for their kivas," Bones added.

"Do you think that's all of them?" Jessie asked. "I mean, all these cliff dwellings should be able to hold a thousand or more, wouldn't you think?"

Bones shrugged. "They've been here for a long time. Maybe this is all that's left."

The Ant Person chittered and jabbed Krueger with his crystal-tipped rod. The message was clear: keep moving.

"You're right. He really doesn't like me." Krueger cast one last, longing glance at the Ant People's home before heading along the ledge to a spot where another gleaming door stood.

The Ant Person placed its hand on the pad and the door slid up. Behind it, a steep passage wound its way upward. The being pointed through the doorway.

"Thank you." Bones didn't know if it understood him, but no harm in being polite.

Amanda pressed her palms together and made a small bow. Surprisingly, the creature inclined its head in response.

"I think he likes girls," Amanda said.

"I don't care what he likes," Padilla said. "I just want to get out of here."

FORTY-EIGHT

"Oh my God!" Matthew stood, gaping at the silver door that barred his way. It shone in the light of his headlamp, smooth and perfect, just like the one he'd found back home. He took out his camera and snapped a few pictures. Maybe his book wasn't dead in the water just yet.

A touch pad was set in the wall to the left of wall. He reached out, then hesitated, his hand hovering an inch above its surface. What if it was dangerous?

"Idiot," he muttered. "The others went through here; so should you."

He'd crept back to the chamber where the masked bodies lay, hoping to sneak up on the Indian, maybe cave his skull in with a rock. When he'd arrived, he found the room empty. He'd followed them down the passage they'd uncovered and ended up here. Obviously, they'd gone through the door. There was nowhere else to go.

Swallowing his fear, he pressed down on the silver pad. A green light shone, swept up and down his body, and then blinked out. A moment later, the door slid open.

He stepped through and followed the passageway, always on high alert for sounds that might indicate someone up ahead. Finally, he saw something in the distance—a greenish light. He turned off his headlamp and crept forward.

The glow grew brighter, and soon he could see that a large, open space lay up ahead. Reaching the end of the passageway, he peered out and gasped.

Below him, a group of aliens, Greys, by the looks of them, milled about. Green light bathed the many dwellings carved in the rock. It was incredible! This was what he'd been searching for!

Awash in the joy of success, he took out his camera and began snapping pictures. Down below, one of the aliens looked up at him, its featureless face betraying no emotion. Matthew kept on taking pictures until something poked him in the side. He looked down to see one of the aliens staring up at him. The creature held a silver rod, like a baton, tipped with a crystal.

"Whoa! You're one of them." Matthew turned and snapped a picture of the alien creature. The thing blinked and took a step back. "Sorry about the flash," Matthew said, "but it's dark in here." He took another picture of the Grey, then returned to photographing the alien dwelling.

Again, the creature jabbed him in the side.

"Look, little guy, take your baton and go practice your twirling, or else I'll throw you over the…"

He stopped in midsentence. The crystal at the end of the rod had begun to glow brightly. So bright, in fact, that Matthew had to shield his eyes.

"I appreciate the light, but it's a little bright."

The light continued to shine brighter.

And with it came heat…lots of it.

Matthew tried to back away but found himself caught between the high ledge and the alien with the thing he now recognized as a weapon.

"Cut it out! I'll leave, all right?" He dared to open his eyes and the light scorched his retinas. His clothing began to smolder, and then the acrid smell of singed hair filled his nose.

When his skin began to sizzle like bacon, he knew it was time to scream.

FORTY-NINE

Hours later they crawled through a narrow crevasse and emerged in a deep valley. The moon hung low on the horizon, casting long shadows across the parched earth. After so long in the chilly caverns, even the scant heat rising from the earth was a comfort.

Bones stretched and looked around. In the distance, he saw the ridgeline that marked the entrance to Carlsbad Caverns. They'd come a long way, and could look forward to a long walk back.

"Too bad it couldn't bring us out a little closer to our destination. I've done enough walking for today." Padilla sucked in a deep breath of night air and let it out slowly. "It was worth it, though. I still can't believe it."

"No one will believe us," Jessie said.

"Welcome to my world," Bones said.

"Tell me about it. I've got a story to write and what do I have to prove it? Nothing." Amanda shook her head. "I suppose I could go back, but it just seems wrong, you know?"

"And dangerous," Bones said. "I don't think visitors would be welcome a second time."

"Speaking of danger," Krueger said, "I guess I need a new identity." He ran a hand through his hair. "Shame. I liked the Roswell museum."

Jessie looked up a Bones. "Do you think we're in danger from ICE?"

Bones considered this. "They know my name for sure. Just to be on the safe side, I think I'll touch base with a friend. She can deal with them. If that doesn't work, I'll personally take care of the sheriff and his friends."

A contemplative silence hung in the air until Jessie forced a laugh.

"On that happy note, what now? Do we just go back to our ordinary lives?"

Bones put an arm around her shoulders. "I hate to tell you, but that's pretty much how these things work."

"So, I sit around for two weeks, waiting for summer

classes to begin, and trying to figure out how I'm going to cover tuition next year."

"I think you've got that covered," Padilla said. "We've got a bit of the Glade Treasure left. Even split five ways, you should be in good shape." He glanced at Bones. "We found it on government land, but I'll bet our resident treasure hunter can help us out there."

Bones nodded. "My uncle owns a casino, so I've got connections."

The others nodded approvingly and resumed their trek back to Bones' truck, but Jessie held him back.

"This is amazing. Thank you!" She lowered her voice. "I don't suppose I can talk you into hanging around for a while?"

"I'll come back for a visit," he said, "but once we've gotten Mari taken care of, I'm going to Vegas."

Jessie stuck out her lower lip. "All alone?"

"My friends are waiting for me there. You can come along if you like. Just remember, what happens in Vegas…"

Jessie laughed. "I don't think that would be much fun for me. Just promise you'll drop by on your way home."

Bones smiled. "It's a plan. Just don't hold me to a date and time. I don't go out of my way to find trouble, but it always seems to find me."

End

ABOUT THE AUTHOR

David Wood is the author of the popular action-adventure series, The Dane Maddock Adventures, and many other works. Under his David Debord pen name he is the author of the Absent Gods fantasy series. When not writing, he co-hosts the Authorcast podcast. David and his family live in Santa Fe, New Mexico. Visit him online at www.davidwoodweb.com.

Made in the USA
San Bernardino, CA
23 September 2016